Jealousy

Novel by:
Demetrice McDonald

Published by DLM Domain Publishing
Published in 2021

This is a work of fiction. Names, characters, places, and incidents either are the product of the author's imagination or are used fictitiously. Any resemblance to actual persons, living, or dead, events, or locales is entirely coincidental.

ISBN 978-1-7348062-0-5

Printed in the United States of America

Dedicated to every person this novel is meant to touch. This is not just a fictional story but the purpose behind it has a true and deeper meaning...

JEALOUSY

DEMETRICE MCDONALD

Chapter One

Warm Welcome

July 2018

It was a hot one today folks,' highs were 98 degrees with a 65 percent humidity, lows tonight will be 75. We are about to...switching stations...static: R&B music plays.

After driving for hours from Trenton, New Jersey, Christina is now close to arriving to her new home in North Charleston, South Carolina. While cruising through the quiet suburb, she glances at the homes around the neighborhood. Christina is still unimpressed by the beautiful large southern style houses, "it looks the same as my last visit two months ago," she says to herself, slightly irritated and grumpy from the long trip. Christina approaches her new home and pulls in the driveway. She parks and waits as her mind drifts away into deep thought.

She smiles. Thinking back to her childhood and growing up in Culver City, California. The pride she felt to be in the heart of screenland. Christina's smile soon fades when she recalls that gut-punched feeling she had the day her father got a better job opportunity in Princeton, New Jersey. Leveling up his position from years of being in financial management to finally becoming a chief financial officer. Christina's parents made the decision to move to Trenton and her father commutes from there to Princeton. The year was 1998, Christina was thirteen years old when this happened. She hated every minute of living in New Jersey and promised herself when she turned eighteen; she would return to California. Though in 2000, the hatred she felt about moving to New Jersey died in the ninth grade at age fifteen, when a New Jersey native turns out to be the love of her life. It was then when Christina started calling Trenton home. However, eighteen years later, in January 2018, like déjà vu, her true love who is now her husband comes to her with news of a better job opportunity. He too has gotten a higher position of authority. Next thing Christina knew, four months later, they were buying their new home. Now that familiar gut-punched feeling has returned, and the anxiety of relocating is in full effect.

She places her hand on her stomach and groans in discomfort. It was then she realized why her anxiety was so intense, Christina has never visited the south. Her first and only visit was two months ago when she and her husband came to buy the house. Christina had plans to vacation places like Miami, Florida, and Atlanta, Georgia, but never follow through with them. Looking back, she notices her procrastinating got the best of her. South Carolina was not even in her vacation plans. The only thing she knows about the state is the hearsay she got from friends, who went there to visit their families, and their responses were never positive. They always came back complaining about how boring it was, and there was not much to do. ***"My grandparents live out near the woods and on a dirt road; you should see how dark it gets at night…creepy."*** Christina recalled her friend Michelle complaining about her "trip to grandma's house." ***"There's nothing but farmers down there. My uncle had me in the hot sun picking vegetables from his huge garden; he was getting ready to sell them."*** Christina remembered how her other friend Jeremy nagged about his trip. ***Those were small towns they talked about***, she thought. She took a moment and realized North Charleston is a large city. It is about the size of Trenton maybe larger, but the size of the town was not Christina's only concern. She left her familiar surroundings and must start over new.

Well, at least there won't be many cold winter days here, she thought, trying to weigh the pros and cons of being in this new city. ***Though, the thought of living in a town surrounded by so much water is disturbing. The Delaware River can't compare to the vast amount that surrounds Charleston.*** "I know hurricanes are common here," Christina thought out loud.

She ends her mini program of "the weather channel" in her mind and soon realizes why she is here, and that is to support her loving husband, who is in the Air Force and stationed at JB Charleston. They wanted to move early and quickly so they would have time getting their new home together before they both became swamped with work. Coming down to South Carolina and taking this job meant a lot to her husband.

Okay, Christina, suck it up and stop being a baby, you probably love it here, she sighs. She tries to calm herself down by listening to the soothing sound of Usher's voice flowing through the air from the radio. For some reason, Christina feels an aggressive uneasiness; that's more than her usual anxiety. She has an overwhelming feeling of something terrible is going to happen to them. ***What if a hurricane comes and destroys our new home, what if another earthquake hits like the one that occurred in Virginia in 2011 and shook the east coast it could happen farther down south next time, what if…no, stop.*** She refuses to let her worries get the best of her. ***I'm overreacting***. Christina snatches the keys out of the ignition and unbuckles her seatbelt.

As soon as she opens the car door, the sweet sound of Usher's voice disappears. She steps out of her air-conditioned, navy blue 2016 Cadillac Escalade into the hot and humid heat. She reaches her arms up and begins stretching and twisting her body to pop her joints and cracks her back. To relax her sore and tired muscles from the long drive. Between getting gas and stopping to eat, it added additional time, making it a thirteen-hour trip. She just wanted to sit down and rest or even better lay down but knowing that wasn't possible to do now because they still needed to unpack. She takes a deep breath and exhales with exhaustion while she looks over her property. She admires all the trees that surrounded the property and continues throughout the entire neighborhood. They were different types and sizes, bringing not only plenty of fresh air but beauty to the small community. The freshly cut lawn and the neighbors on both sides of her home have done an excellent job keeping their lawn up. ***It is beautiful and peaceful down here, no drivers honking their car horns, no sirens blaring. The sound of birds chirping and the leaves blowing on the trees from the breeze …just tranquil, but the summertime here is scorching. I'm glad I dressed for this weather***. She thought as she begins fanning herself. Wearing a red tank top and white Bermuda shorts, it is July, and even though evening hours were approaching, the humidity was intense.

JEALOUSY

The moisture in the air was dense and muggy.

After being in the heat for three minutes, Christina can feel the beads of sweat forming on her forehead and sweat pouring down her back, but the view of her new home takes her mind off the heat. In front of her is a beautiful two-story house made up of chardonnay colored ledge stones with black sidings, shutters, and a charcoal-colored rooftop. Their large porch was complemented with an old-fashioned porch swing giving it a southern appeal, the dream home she and her husband always wanted. Even though they lived in a luxury one-bedroom apartment in Trenton, it is safe to say a three-bedroom two-story house is an upgrade. As she admires her home, she realizes it is taking her husband a little longer to pull up right behind her as he was supposed to. Christina opens the car door and leans in to grab her rose gold colored smartphone, that was sitting in the cupholder and calls him.

"Hello," he answered.

"Where are you?" she asked.

"Not far, I'm coming. I just…HEY, WHAT THE FUCK!" **Horn blaring**

Christina jumped from his sudden outburst. "What happened?!" she asked.

"This dumbass cut me off! Almost ran me off the road! New York tags, what the hell is he doing down here?" He asked rhetorically then huffs. "Anyway baby, I'm on my way. I need to get some gas."

"Honey, you couldn't do that afterwards? We got a lot to do and have to get that rental truck back on time or we will be paying for an additional day."

"I know, and yes I have to get gas now. I'm riding on fumes."

"Hurry up please. It's 6:30 pm, we have to unpack and get the truck back by 9:00 pm."

"Yes ma'am." he answered sarcastically.

Christina sucked her teeth. "Alright bye."

He chuckles. "Bye."

Christina shakes her head in amusement, knowing them, things happen like this all the time. So, as she waits for his arrival, she heads inside their new home. When she walks in, she immediately notices that the furniture was delivered on time and laid out how she wanted but thinks she may have to rearrange a few things. Christina turns the thermostat to 65 degrees and makes her way upstairs. Wanting to check all the rooms and make sure nothing is missing or damaged. Christina stared at the empty, freshly painted walls and imagined filling the space with wedding photos and one-day pictures of her children. She sighed at the thought of having kids, hoping one day she and her husband will start a family. As Christina continued, she entered the master bedroom and saw the king-size bed there and already assembled. She was happy to know that all that was needed for her to do was make it up. ***I am so excited to put on the brand-new king size comforter set I bought to celebrate our new home. I have three to choose from black and gold, purple and white.*** While Christina debated on which color comforter set to use first, she's interrupted by knocks on the front door. She moves quickly towards the door; surprised by the knocking.

"WOW, DON'T TELL ME YOU LOST YOUR KEYS TOO!"

Christina yelled while coming down the stairs hoping her husband would hear her, but when she opens the door, standing there was not her husband. It was a tall, dark complexion man. He stood about six foot four inches and slim; his skin was a shade lighter than the black shirt he was wearing. He was a West African man. When he saw Christina, who is a petite five foot three inches, slender, chocolate brown complexion, and with long hair that she placed neatly in a tight ponytail. He looks at her as if she is the most amazing woman he has ever seen.

"Oh hi…can, I help you," asked Christina startled that it was not her husband.

"My name is Agali Sawadogo; I live next door." His accent was strong, like he came to America for the first time that same day. "I saw your car outside and felt it would be polite to introduce myself to my new neighbor."

"Nice to meet you, I'm Christina; I'm glad you stopped by."

"Trust me. The pleasure is all mine. Christina is a beautiful name." He looks at her in awe. "Are you moving in today, do you need any help carrying boxes?"

"Yes, I am, but I don't need help, thank you; I'm just waiting on my husband to arrive."

"Oh, you're married," Agali said with disappointment.

"Yes, I am." Christina smiled.

"Marriage is a wonderful thing. I hope I find a wife as beautiful as you are someday." Agali continues to stare at Christina deeply.

"Aww, thank you." She let out a bashful giggle.

"You are welcome. So, what part of Africa are you all from?"

"Oh, I'm not African, well what I mean is I was born in America, I'm Afro-American, and my husband is Puerto Rican."

After Christina said the race of her husband was Puerto Rican, Agali's demeanor changed drastically. He could not believe who he thought was the most beautiful black woman he had ever seen, had a Hispanic spouse. He felt robbed, like a thief just stolen something near and dear to him.

"Is something wrong," asked Christina when she noticed his disturbed expression.

"No," Agali answered defensibly, trying to look unbothered by what he just heard.

The rumbling of the moving truck approaches. Christina's husband pulls in the driveway behind the Escalade and parks. He slowly climbs out of the truck. His muscles were also sore from the long trip and were dreading the additional work of unpacking. He saw Christina talking to Agali, wondering who he could be, and quickly made his way over to them.

"There's my husband now; you can meet him,"

"I'm sorry I just remember I have something important to do at home," Agali said while in a hurry to leave. The last thing Agali wanted to do was to meet her Hispanic husband or the thief as he refers him to.

"Okay, but it will just take a second to say hi, here he comes now."

Christina's husband is six feet tall, muscular, with an even brown skin tone like he just stepped out of a tanning salon. His hair was black and cut close military-style. Christina looks at him, smiles and continues with the introduction.

"Babe, I want you to meet Agali Sawadogo, he is our neighbor and Agali, meet Torres Sosa."

"How are you doing, sir, nice to meet you," Torres greeted.

Torres holds out his hand to shake, but Agali is reluctant to take it. Like he was disgusted by the sight of him. Even though Agali immediately grew a hate for Torres. He didn't want to offend Christina. He did not agree with her choice in men, but Agali could not help that he was fond of her. Agali shakes Torres' hand and gives a broad smile showing the massive gap in the top row of his front teeth.

"You are a fortunate man to have a wife like her," Agali said, although his words were full of resentment.

"Thank you, you're right, I am." Torres smiles and looks at Christina.

"That's sweet." She began blushing; all she could do was smile at all the flattery she received.

"I must be going now," Agali said as he rushes towards home.

"Ok, hope we can talk later," Torres yelled as Agali reaches his yard.

"Yes, I hope." Agali responds.

Agali turns and walks back towards his house, which is also two stories, made up of fiber cement sidings; it was grey and an older build than Torres and Christina's home. It didn't have the large porch, but a small set of steps and a platform in front of his front door. When Agali reached his door, he looked back over at the couple then hurried into his home.

"Alright, baby, let's get this truck unpacked, Vámonos!" Torres shouted, then slaps his wife's behind. Christina giggles.

Torres goes and opens the truck, and it was then when Christina realized she forgot to get the suitcases from the car. She goes and unpacks the Escalade while Torres sets up the unloading deck to the truck and climbs inside. Christina takes the luggage into the living room and quickly goes back outside to help Torres unpack the truck. Torres takes the small boxes and pushes them to the front so Christina can reach them. As the couple playfully unloads the truck, Christina places a somewhat heavy box on top of the heavy box Torres is already holding, she laughs when his legs buckle from the weight. Unknowingly they are being watched. Agali glares out his kitchen window, still upset about Christina's choice of husband. Agali has dated American black women before, but since he is an abusive and very controlling man, the relationships never last long. Of course, Agali doesn't see himself as the problem. He feels if women weren't so stupid, he would not have to control their every move, and Christina marrying Torres makes his beliefs about how dumb women are even stronger.

"Here is a beautiful woman, who could pass as a Nigerian princess, is with not even an American black man but a Puerto Rican. She should be with me!"

He utters in rage as he watches Christina and Torres play around while they unpack. Torres grabs her in his arms and spins her around.

"Look at him showing off," Agali grumbled.

Agali glared out the window for over an hour. His heart swelled up with anger as he watched the couple unload each box or bag from the truck. He grunts from the pain of jealousy in his chest as he watches Torres grabbing Christina from behind and kisses her neck.

Surprisingly, the couple never notices his glares; they played and giggled like teenagers experiencing love for the first time. The sight of it all was sickening to Agali. He steps away from the window and goes over to the refrigerator and pulls out a twelve-ounce salmon fillet; he begins cutting it into four pieces.

"I shouldn't have to cook my dinner; that's what a wife is for," he grumbled.

Agali felt by age 30 he would be married and started a family. He is 40 years old now, still unwed and no kids. The thought of still being alone angered him more. Agali stomps around in the kitchen as he continues preparing his meal. He pulls out a baking pan and aluminum foil and places the fillet inside the pan. Then he grabs his seasonings, red wine vinegar, virgin olive oil, and a bag of rice. He puts a pot of water on the stove and waits for it to boil. Agali sets the oven to 400 degrees and preps his fish. He places the fish in the oven and adds the rice to the boiling water.

Agali can hear the couple's laughter, causing his rage to grow stronger. While his food is cooking, he goes back to the window to continue to watch the couple but notices they have finished unpacking. Christina is carrying the last small box inside. Torres closes the back of the truck and checks the latch making sure it is secure, then goes and hops in. Agali watches as Christina goes inside, and Torres pulls out the driveway and drives away. Christina quickly places the last box beside the door, locks the front door, hops in the Escalade, and follows her husband to the truck rental store. Agali steps away from the window; he goes over to the stove and turns off the pot of rice and pulls the fish back out of the oven and tosses it into the trash. The pain in his chest had moved to his stomach, and Agali had utterly lost his appetite. He rests his hands on the countertop and hangs his head low. He inhales and exhales slowly and glares at the floor as he begins to get lost in thought. ***They shouldn't be together; they can't possibly be happy. Anybody that tries so hard to look happy is hiding something.***

"I mean who flirts while unpacking?"

Agali asked out loud as if he would get an answer to that question. He continues to go over in his thoughts of him and Christina being together. The feelings he has for her were confusing. He didn't know whether it was love at first sight or the fact that he didn't want Torres to have her. Either way, something needed to be done.

"I must make her mine," he whispered.

WARM WELCOME

Torres and Christina returned home. They were both exhausted after such a long day. "Babe let's finish unpacking in the morning," Torres said as he and Christina entered the master bedroom.

"I'm way ahead of you, I was thinking we can finish unpacking tomorrow afternoon and sleep in late," Christina responded.

"Mm-hmm sounds good to me," Torres said as he kicked off his shoes. Torres and Christina worked together, making up the bed with their new black and gold sheets and comforter set.

"Yuck, I need a shower I feel so sticky," Christina said while rubbing her hands up and down her arms.

"Me too," Torres agreed.

They both showered together, stayed undressed, then laid together in the middle of the king-sized bed. Torres laid flat on his back while Christina laid on top of him, rubbing her face against his muscular peck, listening to the sound of his heartbeat was very relaxing to her.

"It's quiet here and peaceful," Torres whispered, breaking the silence in the room.

"Yeah, it is," Christina sighed.

"If I haven't said it before, thank you for doing this, I know how you hated leaving, but this job could mean a lot more money and benefits, not to mention the position itself is an honor." Torres softly spoke as he rubs her back then moves his hand down to her buttocks.

"I know this opportunity means a lot to you" … Christina pauses to gather her thoughts. "You don't have to thank me; I'll do anything for you."

"Yes, I know, and I'll do anything for you too."

Torres kissed Christina on the top of her head and held her tightly. Christina thought she should say more to discuss how she didn't care about more money. It wasn't like they were struggling to make ends meet. Money couldn't replace the comfort of her family and friends. Christina knew she wouldn't be able to see them as often as she used to and groans from that thought.

"What's wrong," Torres asked when he heard her moan.

"Nothing…I'm just a little sore that's all," She lied. She didn't want to sound like a whiny or nagging wife.

"Tomorrow, I'll give you a full body massage," Torres uttered as he began to fall asleep. She kissed his chest, squeezed him tightly, then drifted to sleep. About an hour had passed, and Christina had fallen into a deep sleep, and fades into a dream,

Christina finds herself surrounded by pitch-black darkness, and the only dim light that was in the room was shining on Agali. Christina looks all around her but can't see anything nor tell where she was; all she saw was darkness and Agali. He stands there, glaring at her. Christina takes steps towards him. As she moves forward, she starts hearing low unidentifiable growls, the sound reminded her of a wolf's snarls but more distorted, the closer she got to Agali the louder they got. Christina was aware not to go near Agali but couldn't stop herself from moving closer to him. It was like she was in a trance, and he was drawing her to him. When she finally reached him, she stared up at him, and he stared down at her, looking directly into each other's eyes. Suddenly, Agali's eyes began changing colors. The white in his eyes was ultimately blood red, and his iris and cornea were white; his pupil was no longer visible. It was as if the iris and cornea were bleached. Christina's breathing quickens as she stares up at Agali's red and white eyes. He huffs and growls and shakes violently. He shrieks an inhumanly loud cry, and his mouth begins to stretch wide like a lion's mouth, Christina could hear the joints in his jaw dislocating, large, long fangs grew from his top and bottom rows of teeth, he lunges toward Christina, grab-

bing her by the arms with both hands; she inhales sharply and starts to shiver in fear. With his long black panther like fangs, he goes to attack.... Christina closes her eyes and screams.

Christina jumps up from the nightmare, shouting and kicking.

"GET OFF ME, GET OFF!" she yelled. Her eyes still closed, she swung her arms, causing herself to get tangled in the sheets. Her fit awoke Torres.

"CHRISTINA! BABY, WHAT'S WRONG!" Torres grabs her and tries to calm her down. "Baby, it's me; it's me. Calm down... you were having a bad dream!"

He pins her to the bed, trying to stop her from fighting. Christina opens her eyes and looks around, gasping for air, trying to catch her breath. Her heart raced, but she was relieved to see that it was just a dream. "Are you alright," Torres asked when he notices Christina's breathing steady. He gets off her and starts unraveling the sheets from around her waist and legs.

"Yes, yes, I'm okay now."

"What happened?" He asked, referring to her nightmare.

"I don't want to talk about it right now; just hold me." She whimpers. Christina lays wrapped in Torres' arms as she tries to go back to sleep.

Chapter Two

On a bright Sunday at 10:00 am, Torres decided to sleep in what he considers late, so that he will be well-rested for his workout to-day with his friend and fellow member of the Air Force. He stretch-es his arms and gives out a long yawn, feeling rejuvenated from his restful night's sleep. Torres sits up on the bed. He turned and saw Christina already up sitting on her side of the bed with her face bur-ied in her hands.

"Good morning, baby," Torres said as he moves over and rubs her back.

"Morning," she answers in a tired tone.

"Did you get any sleep?" Torres asked, noticing Christina's weariness.

"Not really." She yawned.

"Are you still having nightmares?"

Two weeks have passed since Christina's disturbing dream with her and Agali, but every night since then, she has had this re-occurring nightmare. This dream was a lot worse than the "Agali nightmare." At least that dream she could explain, but not this one. In these nightmares, she is still surrounded by the same darkness. However, what she saw in the dim light was no longer Agali; there lurking in the dark is a being the size and shape of a Kodak bear. Its whole body has long black shiny hair, and it was coarse like a lion's mane, it had a nose like a pig's snout, long fangs on the top and bottom rows of its teeth like a black panther, and six-inch-long claws. What made it even more frightening were its piercing glowing red eyes. Its eyes were not red and white like Agali's were, but completely bright blood red. In all her dreams, it crouches down on all fours as if it is getting ready to attack. Completely horrified of it, Christina refuses to talk about it. Even though she knows better; her being a psychiatrist, and always encouraging the people she counsels to speak about their problems; she's being hypocritical and ignores hers. Christina usually tells her husband everything, but not this. Most of the time, talking to him was comforting, but with all her education on the human mind, even she couldn't explain why she is dreaming about an animal or a thing she's never seen before, not in person nor on TV, nor anywhere else. If it were an animal, then there would be an explanation. Individual animals are a form of symbolism in dreams; what they are doing or the color of them gives a more detailed meaning. A general animal, like a bear, symbolizes a person's ability to self-analysis. Of course, that "thing" in Christina's dreams was no bear, just the shape and size of one. How was her mind able to come up with such an image and why has she been dreaming about it every night for the past two weeks? How it came to her is a mystery she's too afraid to solve. Christina even tried putting herself in the client's shoes, thinking about what she would tell someone who was having this problem. Doing this, she came up with a professional answer such as dreams are a mystery, and whatever emotional state the person is in can have a significant effect on what they dream. The problem is the beast presence in her dreams are too real, some nights, Christina swears it was breathing on her, and that feeling wakes her up. Thinking it could have been Torres sleeping on top of her as he sometimes does. Only to be disappointed to wake and see he's laying facing away from her. Christina tries to block any memories of that creature, hoping soon the nightmares would stop on their own the same way they started and lies about what happened in her dreams.

"Were you drowning again?" Torres asked. It was one of the lies Christina told him.

"Uh yeah," she replied.

"You're probably dreaming about drowning because we're surrounded by all this water, just relax." Torres rubs her shoulders.

"Yes, you're right; I've been stressed and experiencing REM sleep, which is causing my nightmares." She said, trying to give him legitimate reasons for her nightmares and lack of sleep.

"Stop talking like a doctor and talk to me like my wife; are you sure you'll alright?"

Christina could hear the concern in his voice, and it upset her that she couldn't just tell him what was wrong. However, she's the professional, and even she couldn't put into words what was wrong, so she doubted he could better explain it. **Maybe I'll tell him later**, she thought.

"Babe, I'm fine…Really," she lied.

"Are you excited about tomorrow?" Christina asked, trying to change the subject.

"There's nothing to be excited about. Before I transferred, they gave me a heads up on what the position required and prepared me for it. So, it will pretty much be the same ole, same…"

"It's not the same," she interrupted. "I'm not just talking about the job, you are going to be around a lot of new people, everything down here is new and different for us."

"Babe, it's not that different you act like we're in China or something," he laughs as he tosses his feet on the floor, sitting right beside her. "Are you worried about adjusting to the area?"

"It's not funny; this is a long way from New Jersey."

"It's going to be fine; we are not that far, just an hour and a half flight, I promise you won't even need a passport," he continued to laugh at Christina exaggeration to moving.

"Oh, very funny, but aren't you concerned about making friends?" Christina could see that Torres wasn't taking her as seriously as she wanted him to, and it was starting to annoy her.

"Not really because my best friend is already here with me, no need to make new ones."

"Oh right, Josh, you two are inseparable, you guys went from going through high school, college, joining the Air Force together, and oh yeah no surprise that you both get the same opportunity to transfer."

"Somebody sounds jealous."

"I am not, so on your first day on this new base, the only person you are going to socialize with is Josh?"

"Pretty much," he answered with a smirk on his face.

"You know what you are?"

"What baby, what am I?" he asked. Torres got up to grab a towel for his shower. He steps out into the hallway looking in the linen closet, causing Christina to speak louder to make sure he heard her.

"You're antisocial! I notice the only friend you have is Josh! You're rude to people, and he's the only one who puts up with it!"

Torres grabbed the first towel his hand touched and rushed back in the bedroom to defend himself.

"Wait, hold up, just because you have a degree in psychology, does not mean you can start labeling people, and I'm not rude, I'm just honest. Besides, you know all the men and women airmen are like family to me. Josh is like the favorite cousin." He responded.

Christina gets up and looks him directly in his face.

"I am not labeling. I'm only observing." She said with a playful but smart attitude.

"So, you observed me being antisocial," he asked mockingly.

"No…well, all I know is, we come to a brand-new city, a perfect time to make friends with new people, and you choose not to."

"I am not, not choosing to make new friends…"

"Huh? Not, Not?" She laughs.

"Hey, you know what I'm saying, ok are you going to go out and make some friends?" he asked.

"I am sort of, at my new job, you know I am going to be counseling abused women and I planned to make friends with them."

"Well, enjoy…. I'm going to hop in the shower want to join me?" he asked with a seductive look.

"Um, as tempting as *that* sounds, I think I'll pass and get some breakfast."

"Ugh, you're cold," Torres mumbled in disappointment.

Christina laughs as she heads downstairs while Torres heads into the bathroom for a cold shower.

Day in and day out, Agali has been fixated on Christina and Torres, watching their every move from when they come from grocery shopping to watching Torres edge up the lawn and Christina plant flowers. He went as far as purchasing a pair of one hundred seventy-four dollars, binoculars so that he can spy through open curtains and open windows. With the constant stalking and obsessing over the couple, Agali grew more annoyed at what he saw. Hoping one day, he would see them argue or act distant towards each other but was disappointed every time. The couple had a happy marriage. Even behind closed doors where no one could see the flaws and the fraudulent acts, some married couples put on in front of others. When they thought no one was looking, they could act "normal," but not Torres and Christina. Even behind closed doors, they were the same. They are compatible and genuinely love each other. Even the moments Agali thought they were fighting would end in laughter or playful jesting towards each other. Agali hated the fact that they were even married, and his hate grew stronger when he discovered they were also happy, but the last straw came Friday morning when Agali went for his morning run, which is something he tries to do at least three times a week.

As he walked past the Sosa's residence, a small pink box bouncing off the light from the streetlights, sticking out the side of their trash can, caught his attention. He looked around to see if anyone was nearby. It was 4:00 am, and most of the neighborhood was still sleeping. He quickly lifted the garbage lid and snatched out the box. It read: `First Response, Early Results Pregnancy Test`. The box carried a little weight to it, so he looked inside it and saw a small white stick. The one line showing in the small box on the stick indicated that the woman who used it was not pregnant.

"He's trying to get her pregnant!"

He growled, the sound of his voice starting a dog to barking. He began breathing heavily and throws the box back in the trash. It was at that moment when Agali knew time was running out, and if he was going to have Christina as his wife, he didn't want her to have a child with Torres; he needs to do whatever it takes to get rid of him.

That Friday morning, Agali walked away from the trash can with burning anger. Instead of his morning run, he paced around the neighborhood in deep thought, wondering what he was going to do to break up Torres and Christina's marriage. ***It's not fair***, he thought. ***She's the perfect woman for me…how did he get her. I never get what I want…it's not fair.*** His mind rambled with thoughts. Around the neighborhood, he circled, two hours have passed as he paced. It begun day breaking, the sun was rising, but Agali didn't notice he had been walking so long. Agali was in full concentration, as his mind took a ride on the emotional roller coaster. He goes from self-pity and sad to vengeful and angry.

"A divorce wouldn't do…" Agali thought out loud. "He would keep coming around trying to get Christina back. He needs to di… YES, that's it!" He exclaimed, not caring if anyone heard him.

He smiles widely as the evil idea forms in his head. He takes off running at full speed towards his home. He bursts in the door and grabs his cordless home phone. Agali called and awoken an old acquaintance of his that Friday morning, demanding that she comes over as soon as she can. Not giving her any reason to why he wants her so urgently, but she knows Agali very well and knows she has no choice but to comply and promises she will visit Sunday.

Christina pours herself a cup of coffee from the fresh pot she made. She goes over to the cabinet, grabs some sugar and powdered creamer then stirs it in. Christina takes a seat at one of the stools in front of the center countertop. She sips on her coffee in hopes it will give her some energy. Her restless nights are not only the result of a tired body but a tired mind as well. She continues to sip as her mind drifts away in thought.

"These past two weeks have been the utmost stressful time of my life." She said to herself. "The move, leaving my family and friends, these terrible nightmares..." She chuckled. "And now I'm talking to myself."

She exhaled, she placed her coffee on the counter and buried her face in her hands. She could hear the footsteps above her moving around in the master bedroom, which was a sign Torres had finished taking his shower and was getting dressed.

"Ugh," Christina groaned. "I got to get breakfast started."

She slowly slid off the stool and went over to the refrigerator. She looked inside it and pondered what would be the quickest and easiest meal to prepare.

"I know Torres will flip if I suggest he have cereal this morning," she sighed. "Ugh, well, omelets aren't much work."

She reached and grabbed the eggs, the pack of diced ham, precut peppers, and shredded cheese, and carries it to the center countertop. She puts her nonstick frying pan on the stove and allows it to heat up. Christina grabs the seasonings and, a large bowl, from the cupboard. Christina grabs a whisk from one of the drawers. She then cracks her eggs and mixes all her ingredients.

The steps of the stairs creaked as Torres walked down them. When she heard Torres coming, she quickly poured some of the blended egg into the pan.

"What's for breakfast?" Torres asked as he entered the kitchen.

"I'm making omelets." Torres goes to the refrigerator and grabs the orange juice.

"Babe, I made coffee," Christina said when she saw the orange juice in his hand.

"Yeah, I saw it, but I'll probably inhale a whole lot of energy drinks at the gym, so I don't need any extra caffeine."

"Okay," Christina responded as she refilled her cup.

"You know while I was in the shower, I thought about what we were talking about earlier; you are upset about coming down here, aren't you?" Torres sits at one of the stools and waits for Christina to answer, but Christina continues to cook using it as an excuse to avoid answering.

"Christina, did you hear what I said?" Torres noticed what she was doing, and it started to bother him.

"Yes, I heard you, but I'm busy."

"You're making eggs; it doesn't take that much effort to make eggs. You're acting differently, and I know something is wrong."

Christina plates the ready omelet she has made and places it in front of him.

"Here…I'm sorry I haven't been myself lately, and I know I've been exaggerating about moving here and stressing about nothing. I remembered you told me when you enlisted that we would be traveling around, and I know this is a great opportunity for us, and I'm sorry if I haven't shown my appreciation."

Christina was so weary that the last thing she wanted to do was fight and thought it would be best to tell Torres everything she felt he needed to hear even though she didn't believe it to be true.

"I'm not looking for an apology. I want to know, are you alright, and are we alright?"

"Yes, we're fine. I'm fine. I promise I'm going to get it together."

She tries to give him a reassuring smile. Torres let out an exaggerated sigh. He knew there was more to what Christina was saying, but also could see Christina wasn't in the mood to talk. He decided to take her word on "getting it together" and said no more about it.

Chapter Three

A white 1998 Windstar van parks in front of Agali's house, and a large dark complexion African woman climbs out of it, and slowly makes her way to the front door. Before she could knock on the door, Agali opens it.

"Welcome, sister, come in." Agali steps back and allows the woman to enter his home. She's nervous as if Agali makes her feel uneasy. The woman is wearing a long black dress. Her hair wrapped up with a black cloth, wrists have gold bracelets about eight on each arm, her ears are full of piercings, and she is wearing a necklace made of bones.

"It's been a while," she begins. "There must be a problem."

"I do have a problem!" Agali said in anger. "I want a wife, and there is one particular woman I have in mind."

"Did you approach her, and she rejected you?" The woman asked.

"No, she is married, and the man she is with does not deserve her."

"Why not, does he cause her harm?" she inquired.

"No, I will let you see for yourself."

Agali took the woman to the window in the kitchen, which is faced to the front of the Sosas' home, giving them a clear view. The woman looks perplexed as to why they are watching out the window.

"How long are we going to be watching, and what is it you want me to see," asked the woman.

"Just wait, you'll see, I'm sure he is going out today, I saw him getting dressed this morning," Agali answered in an irritated tone.

"Who?" She asked.

"HUSH WOMAN AND WAIT!" Agali yelled, his patience was getting short.

About thirty minutes later, Josh, Torres' best friend, pulls up into the Sosas' driveway, driving a black 2017 Nissan Titan pick-up truck and blows the horn. Josh is six feet two inches, same chocolate complexion as Christina, Afro-American with muscular arms. He put on a few pounds in the stomach area, which faded the six-pack he once had, and he also has the same military-style haircut. Torres is in the kitchen, putting his dish in the sink and quickly swallows down his orange juice. He heard the horn, heads to the door and goes out on the porch to wave to his friend to let him know he's on his way.

"Baby, that's Josh. I gotta go!" Torres called.

Torres has on his muscle shirt and basketball shorts with the Air Force decals on it. He's ready to hit the gym. Christina runs out on the porch in her robe to kiss her husband goodbye and waves at Josh.

JEALOUSY

"THERE YOU SEE!" Agali said with excitement, startling the woman with his sudden outburst.

"Those two are married," Agali said with a sour expression on his face, disgusted by the thought of them being together.

"Where are they from, are they from South Africa?" She asked, noticing Torres's skin tone, thinking he looked biracial.

"They are not African," Agali said as he walks away from the window. "She's an American, and the husband is a Puerto Rican."

"A Puerto Rican," she repeated. She watches as Torres gets in the truck, and Josh drives off.

Agali goes into a drawer of one of the end tables and pulls out a wooden pipe, a box of matches, and cut pieces of tobacco. He took a cut piece of tobacco and stuffed it in his wood pipe; he then strikes a match and lit his pipe and started sucking on the pipe, drawing the smoke in his mouth, and letting the smoke exhale through his nose as he stares blankly in deep concentration.

"Why did you call me," the woman asked nervously, awaiting the reply.

Agali broke his blank stare and looked directly at the woman. The woman's heart pounded; she knew his reason for calling her wasn't good. It's not like they were close friends. She thought Agali was going to go off in a rant since he does have a very hostile nature, but surprisingly he had a depressed look on his face and sadly answered.

"I need you to get rid of him and make her fall in love with me," he replied. The woman took a moment to search her thoughts. She knew Agali was serious and she had to give him something or else he'll try to get rid of her. Finally, she spat out the first thing she could think.

"The problem you seem to be having is the jealousy of an interracial couple" .... she paused when she saw the glare Agali gave her.

"I am not jealous of them; it just makes good sense for her to be with her kind."

Agali spoke affirmingly. He now genuinely believed that breaking Torres and Christina up and making Christina his, was the right thing to do.

"Yes, of course," the woman agreed out of fear. "The only reason I brought it up is that I recently came across a form of witchcraft where you can call certain spirits in its rawest state."

"What spirits, there are different ones?" Agali started wondering how this could help him.

"Yes, I know, but there is a spirit of jealousy that you can call, and after it comes, it does not dwell in the individual alone, but others join it, leaving the person in a vulnerable state."

"How do you call them?" Agali asked with his interest, suddenly struck.

"There's a small ritual you must do, and you will need some items, but I must warn you, it is dangerous, not many have tried it, and someone always perishes when used."

"That is what I want..." Agali said, his eyes focused on her with an evil glare. "I want him to perish." A sick and twisted smile came upon his face.

"BUT ARE YOU SURE?!" ...the woman cried in terror. I thought you wanted to control them, make him divorce her, and make her fall in love with you?"

"THAT'S NOT ENOUGH!" He yelled. "Her husband needs to die. I don't want him around at all." He said through gritted teeth.

"Look," she swallowed hard. "I know you want her to be yours, but you have to understand when that spirit comes in a life-threatening matter. It will possess that person, and their death will be slow, and painful…no one deserves this."

When she said that out loud, she realized she made a huge mistake telling Agali about it at all. She knows what kind of person he is. She swallowed hard again, choking back tears. She then cried out,

"I'm sorry I brought it up! I'll look for another spell, I'll..."

"NO!" he interrupted, "THAT IS THE SPELL I WANT GO AND BEGIN IT NOW! Those bones can't protect you; I know your weakness, so you will do as I say."

Agali is in her face with a deranged and obsessive look in his eyes, the woman steps back away from him and says,

"I will get you the supplies and tell you how to do it, but I will not perform it, I don't care what you do to me."

"Well, go and get them." He waved her away. She nodded and quickly made her way out the front door.

Chapter Four

"Yo', Josh, where are we going; I thought we were going to the base to hit the gym?" Torres asked when he noticed they passed the interstate.

"We are man. I just got to make a quick stop at the church," Josh replied.

"The church," Torres asked, surprised.

"You know Sarah's father is a pastor. She wants me to deliver him some chocolate chip cookies she baked last night. It's her way of trying to smooth things over for skipping church this morning. She said these were his favorite," Josh explained.

"Oh yeah, I forgot Sarah was from Charleston."

"Yep, this country life is home sweet home to her. She lit up when I told her about transferring here."

"I wish Christina was as excited, but why your wife could not take the cookies herself, we got a long drive to the base."

"Because she asked if I could do it, her and an old childhood friend she ran into yesterday, had breakfast together and made an appointment today to get a tan and wax, besides it's not that long of a drive it's like 25 minutes away."

"I don't get why some white women love getting tans, everybody trying to be dark," Torres remarked.

"Don't be talking about my wife." Josh looked at him with an *"I can't believe you just said that"* look.

"I was just making a statement, man, calm down." Torres shook his head to show what he said was not that serious. Josh sucked his teeth.

While they drove, Torres gazes out the window taking in the sights. School hasn't started back yet, so there were a lot of kids out expressing their freedom from class assignments and homework. He watched as the kids of all ages riding their bikes, scooters, rollerblades. Laughing, enjoying the beautiful summer day. Watching the kids brought sadness to him. He wants children of his own, and Christina was having difficulties getting pregnant. They have tried different things and seen specialists and still were unsuccessful. Although he doesn't blame her, he can't help but feel like they are failing in their marriage because their family isn't complete. He talks to his wife about everything, but not this; he won't let her know his true feelings of hurt and frustration from every negative pregnancy test. He smiles, swallows his pain, and tells his wife, "it's okay; it's going to happen one day."

The navigation system lets them know they have arrived at their destination. Josh checks the address Sarah wrote down for him to the address on the building.

"You haven't been here before?" Torres asked.

"Yeah, I have, but I didn't drive, nor was I paying attention.

Since this is Sarah's hometown, and she knows this place like the back of her hand, I let her take the wheel." Torres turns his attention back towards the building.

The church was a one-story building, but the attic it had made it look two stories. It was all white with a gray rooftop; the windows stained with biblical images, and it had a 1950s structure with a spotty paint job done by an amateur. The name of the church was in black letters on a white painted pine board mounted on the front wall of the church. It read: Free Rock Baptist Church of God.

"This is it though, I remembered the building, are you coming in?" asked Josh.

"Yeah, why not."

"Hey, maybe while you're here, you can tell the father a confession," Josh joked.

"Catholics make confessions, not Christians," Torres corrected.

"Oh yeah," Josh remembered.

"Man, do you pay attention at all while you're in church?"

"Yes, I do. I was joking. I was just testing you."

"Yeah, right."

"I was, I know, the difference between Catholics and Christian. Anyway, going to church is going to be an ongoing thing now; we couldn't make it this morning, so this is Sarah's way of apologizing. We have no choice but to go next Sunday." Josh groaned.

"Wow, that's some faith you have, you're upset about going to church," Torres remarked.

"I know you are not talking; you and Christina should come with us."

"I don't go to everybody's church," Torres commented as he looked up at the church.

"I'm offended by that; this is my father-in-law you're talking about."

"Calm down, sensitive. I don't know. I'll talk to Christina about it,"

Torres laughs at his joke towards Josh being sensitive. Josh jumped at Torres in a playful threat as if he was going to hit him. They laugh as they climbed out of the truck. Josh and Torres went up four red-bricked steps and entered the church through the double door entrance; the inside of the church had a better appearance than the outside of it. The walls were wood stained, identical sets of pews on each side of the church; in front three steps lead up to a huge altar, with the podium in the middle, behind was a sizeable king-like chair, "the pastor's chair," and on each side of it, two sets of chairs for the elders and visiting pastors. In the very back was a large curtain, almost reaching the ceiling and an inch from the floor, covering the baptism pool.

"I think Sarah said his office is this way the last room at the end."

Josh points down a wide hallway filled with paintings with biblical images on it. Each reflected passages from the bible; some were famous stories like David and Goliath and Jonah and the great fish. Torres looks at the images in amazement as he remembered the stories. The illustrations in the paintings were incredible. Torres wonder the identity of the artist who captured these stories on the canvas. The one that stood out to him the most was a story he remembered learning from his grandmother. Torres was not much of a churchgoer. He was raised in a family with different religious views. His grandparents and mother were Christians, but his father was Catholic, and his mother chose to convert to her husband's beliefs. The painting that Torres found interesting was not the most famous. It showed a group of men on the left side, one man in front of them, who the artist meant him to be the Son of God and before him another man who fell to the ground to worship him. In front of them were structures that looked like tombs. At the bottom right of the canvas were pigs falling off a cliff and into water. The painting could only vaguely demonstrate all that happened in that story, but Torres still figured it out. ***I remember this story,*** He thought. The pigs are what jogged his memory.

The man on the ground was possessed, and then the unclean spirits inside him begged Jesus if they could go into the pigs. The thought of how that image stuck out the most gave him an unexpected chill down his spine.

"You alright, man"?

Josh asked when he notices his friend had stopped walking. Torres snaps out of his trance,

"Yeah, I'm good."

He took one last look and continued. They reached the last room, and Josh knocks on the door. A man's voice answers, "Come in." Josh and Torres walk in; inside are two men.

One sits behind a large desk, dress in a black robe, the pastor of the church, and Josh's father-in-law. He was a large man with pale skin. It seemed like the pastor doesn't expose himself to any sunlight often. He had cropped brown hair that shows more grey than brown, with a matching goatee. The other sits in a chair up against the wall, wearing a light blue shirt and khaki pants. They both were Caucasian men; the other had an athletic build, short dark brown hair, and his skin looked as if it glowed, and it had no flaws.

"Oh, Josh, what a pleasant surprise, and who is the gentleman you brought with you," asked Josh's father-in-law.

"This is Torres Sosa, don't you remember, he was the best man at the wedding."

"Nobody remembers the best man, only the bride, and groom," Torres said with an embarrassed smile. He remembered talking to Josh's father-in-law at the wedding and was surprised he had forgotten him already.

"Torres, this is Pastor John Henry." Josh reintroduced.

"Please, call me John, nice to meet you again, Torres," he reaches out to shake his hand.

"You to sir," Torres responds.

"I'd like you both to meet Deacon Jacobs." Pastor Henry announced.

He looks more like a model than a deacon in the church, Torres thought as he directed his attention to him.

"You can call me Paul if you like," he said.

"Paul, this is my son-in-law Josh and his friend Torres." Pastor Henry continued.

"Nice to meet you," Paul shakes their hands.

"Josh don't think I didn't notice you and Sarah's absence at this morning's service", scold Pastor Henry. "Also, the last time you were here, you dozed off during my sermon."

Josh nervously grinned. "I'm sorry, sir, that's why I'm here. Sarah wanted me to bring you these cookies she baked. They're your favorite."

"This was nice, thank you, but it doesn't change things I expect to see you both next Sunday and every night of service we have. Coming to church is not a punishment; you should enjoy going and want to come, not see it as a chore."

"I know we will be here bright and early next time," Josh promised.

"Ok, please stay and have a cookie." Everyone grabbed one except Paul. "You are welcome to have one, Deacon," Pastor Henry said.

"No, thank you," Paul answered.

Secretly Paul has been fasting for the past 39 days. He had been told by God to go on the fast, and it had to last 40 days, that day was his last, and he didn't want all the work he did to sacrifice to be ruined by a cookie. He didn't understand why he had to endure the fast but, with his trust in the Lord, he obeyed. Torres stared at him, and Paul smiled back.

"So, do you fellas have any plans today?" Paul asked, breaking Torres' stare.

"We need to hit the gym to prepare for tomorrow," Josh answered.

"What happens tomorrow?" Paul probed.

"We're in the Army Air Force we transferred down here from New Jersey," Josh answered.

"We have a certain weight we need to maintain, and as you can see, Josh put on a few pounds." Torres chimed in. Pastor Henry and Paul both chuckled at Torres's remark.

"Aye, man, I can still outrun you." Josh boosted.

"Yeah, whatever." Torres rolled his eyes.

"Well, I hope you two have a good day and tell my daughter her cookies were delicious, and I'll call her later," said Pastor Henry.

"I will. You guys have a good day as well," said Josh as he and Torres were leaving out the room.

Paul waved goodbye at Torres, and Torres responded, but as soon as the door closed, Torres wipes the fake smile off his face and expresses how he feels.

"Since when did they start electing male models to be deacons of the church?"

"What?" Josh asked, confused by the question.

"You saw that guy; he didn't want any of your wife's cookies; I guess he was watching his figure."

"Wow, talking about a man of God... You know you're going to hell, right?" Josh laughed.

"Whatever man, I'm just voicing my opinion, what's wrong with that." Torres defended.

"By calling him a male model. I think you got a crush on him; don't worry, I won't tell Christina." Josh laughed a little harder.

"Shut up! You not even funny." Josh snicker at Torres's seriousness to his comment. Torres shakes his head.

"What's wrong?" Josh wondered.

"I don't know. It's just; I've seen so many people like that before. You mostly see happy, have it together people talk about God, where are the ones suffering and saying I still believe?"

"Real talk Torres, you just met that man, how you know he's "happy and have it together" looks can be deceiving; besides, why you hatin' on that man?"

"Never mind forget it," Torres didn't want to get into what he was feeling; he couldn't explain why he felt that way. "Let's go, man." Torres sighed.

As they continued, Josh walked ahead, still amused by Torres' comments. Torres slowly trailed behind as he thought about Paul and wondered about his own beliefs, and wanted to ask Paul some questions, but as Josh walks out the door, he decided against it and quickly caught up with his friend.

Chapter Five

The Spell

Later that night, the large woman returned to Agali's house.

"What took you so long!" he shouted out impatiently.

"Here you are," she said as she handed him a sack.

Agali snatches it from her and begins pulling out the items. There were two jars.

"That's possum's blood, and the other is dirt from a newborn's grave," she said.

"A newborn's grave?" He asked, puzzled.

"Yes, if a mother has a child that dies moments after it was born. It's the dirt from the grave where they buried it; it's potent in witchery," she explained.

Agali also pulls out of the sack a stone bowl, two black candles, and a small cement spreader tool. "Is this all I need?" he asked.

"Yes, that is all the materials you need." She stops and slowly reaches into her bag. She takes out a piece of paper with the spell written on it and looks at Agali. "Here's the spell," she whispered.

"Now, how does this work?" Agali asked, again snatching the paper from her.

"All you have to do is at 3:00 am, light both candles and mix the blood and dirt. Then read the spell."

"What is this for," he holds up the cement spreader tool.

"After you mix the dirt and blood, you use that to spread on the floor or ground so the person you cursed can stand on it. Like if you were to spread it on the ground in front of their door."

"No, I can't risk her standing on it. I'll invite them over and lure Torres on it." Agali smiled.

"My work here is done; now, I must go."

"Yes, you may leave, thanks for your help,"

Agali said with a sneer. The woman lowered her head in shame and started walking towards the front door, dragging her feet like a child who was just grounded and sent to their room. She looked at Agali one last time as she left out the door. He didn't notice. Agali just stood there smiling as he read over the spell.

At 2:50 am, Agali began preparing for his ritual. He went into his bedroom and pulled out a small foldable table and a small cut piece of black cloth. He drapes the fabric on top of the table; it's stained with melted wax because he has used it before in other rituals. He sat the stone bowl in the middle of the table and placed the two jars, one on each side of it. He waits until it is precisely 3:00 am, then he lit the candles. He put the newborn's grave dirt in first then poured in the blood. He pours it in slowly, making sure he doesn't spill a drop. He gets his wooden spoon and starts mixing. The stench of the blood and dirt causes him to wrinkle his nose. He continues until it is thoroughly mixed. He opens the paper she gave him; the ritual chant was in French. Agali started thinking about his childhood and being raised in Nigeria. English was his first language. His parents were from Burkina Faso and were fluent in French, which caused Agali to grow up bilingual. He grew up speaking to his parents in French but was taught in English at school. He also picked up on other languages as well. He always felt the more languages you know; the more people are available to you. He ended his daydream of the thought of how smart he was and returned his focus on the spell. It was now five minutes after 3:00 am, and he knew he had no time to waste. The spell read :

Appelant les esprits sombres qui vivent dans des endroits secs je dois une mission qui peut-être votre oasis, venu en cette heure il Ya quelqu'un vous doit dévorer. [Calling the dark spirits that live in dry places I have a mission that can be your oasis, come this hour, there's a soul you must devour].

He begins to chant; the instructions are to repeat the chant three times. As he begins chanting it a second time, he starts to hear a growling sound. He stops and looks around but doesn't see anything and continues. He does the third and final chant. He felt a breeze blow in the draft less room, neither window nor door was open, the wind blows out the candles. The growl he heard earlier was even louder than before. He listened to what sounds like footsteps stampeding down his hall. His bedroom door burst open, and a strong force broke through the window, glass shatters on the floor as if something left to do its task. Agali was startled at first but then smiles.

"It has begun."

JEALOUSY

~Earlier that night at 11:30pm~

"How did you hurt your shoulder again?" asked Christina while sitting on top of Torres' back, giving him a massage.

"Aw baby, I told you, Josh was showing off by how much he could bench, and I took on his challenge." Torres moaned.

"So, your male ego almost caused you to break something, okay, I get it now," she said sarcastically.

Torres sucks his teeth. "Ha-ha, very funny…hey, remember I told you about that guy me and Josh met today?"

"What guy, Sarah's dad?"

"No, not him, the other one I told you how weird he was."

"Oh yeah, why was he so weird?"

"He just was, I can't explain it," Torres grumbled.

"Honey, why are you so suspicious of everybody, there are good people out there believe it or not." Christina rubbed his shoulder with a little more pressure.

"I'm not suspicious, and I know there are some good people, but I also know there are some fake people out there too."

Christina licked her lips and smiled. "Oh yeah, I forgot to tell you."

"Tell me what," Torres looks over his shoulder.

"That Deacon called me and asked were you and Josh coming over to the church. He wanted to be there so he could fake like he was such a good Christian…he just wanted to piss you off." Christina burst out laughing.

Torres turns over quickly, knocking Christina off his back. "Instead of being a smart ass, I know something better you can do."

She grins. "And what's that," she asked.

Torres leans towards her and starts sucking and kissing on her neck. Christina softly moans as she starts to feel sexually aroused. She lies on her back, and Torres spreads her legs apart and lies between her thighs then kisses her passionately. Christina stops him.

"Mm, but what about your shoulder?"

"I think I can push through." They laughed, then continue kissing.

As the intimate and romantic encounter takes place, watching from his window into theirs, using his binoculars to get a good look, is Agali, glaring as his heart races. "She will be mine soon," he muttered.

Chapter Six

"Welcome, everyone. I would like you all to meet Dr. Christina Sosa. She is going to be our new counselor transferring here from New Jersey," announced Amy Simpson.

Amy, a chubby lady with rosy cheeks, glasses, and red hair, she would remind you of a female version of Santa Claus, or even better, Mrs. Claus. Amy is the coordinator and founder of the "Loving hearts" organization for battered and abused women.

"Dr. Sosa, would you like to say something to the group?"

"Well, I feel I should let everyone know a little about myself." Christina decided to stand in front of her seat for her brief presentation.

"Hello everyone, you already know my name, so I'll start with a little background about myself. I'm originally from California, actually, but my family moved to New Jersey when I was 13 years old. I went to Kean University and received my Bachelor's in Psychology and my Master's in Counseling. I received my PH.D. in Personality and Social Psychology at Princeton University. What inspired me to go into this field is the experience I had in working with abused individuals while I was still in high school. I used to volunteer at a church where the pastor counseled victims of drugs and alcohol abuse; my big and important assignment was to serve refreshments."

She chuckled. Some members of the group and Amy politely laughed at the weak joke Christina made.

"I still listened to their sessions and watched how he helped turn their lives around, and ever since then, helping people has been a passion of mine."

"Wow," said Amy moved by Christina's expression.

"Does anyone have any questions for me?"

Christina asked the small crowd in front of her; there were only ten women in the room, including Christina and Amy. The eight abused women filled the room with different personalities. Four of them appeared as they were happy to be there; three of the others were the complete opposite. They looked like they were forced to come, which is unlikely because this is a voluntary event. The look on their faces had a mixture of bitterness and depression. The last girl acted as if she was suffering from a strong case of paranoia. She looked frightened, constantly looking over her shoulder as if she believes her attacker will appear at any minute.

Christina noticed her right away. She scanned the room, making mental notes of each person, trying to guess their temperaments during the session.

All eight of the women did share one thing in common. They were all scarred and bruised. Two of the women from the "*happy to be here*" group had one of their arms in a sling. The scared one had crunches lying beside her and a cast on her right leg.

"I got a question?" said a girl from the "*I don't want to be here*" group with her hand slightly rose.

She had dirty blonde hair and fair skin, which made that shiner around her eye very noticeable; she appeared to be a lot younger than the other women. She was wearing a hoody that was two sizes too big, pants were dirty, and the Reeboks she was wearing have seen better days.

"Yes," Christina answered.

"Sosa," so are you half Mexican or something?" she asked in a nasty tone.

"Um," Christina began surprised by the question. "No, I'm all Afro American, my husband is Puerto Rican, and Sosa is my married name."

"Oh," she responded as if she didn't care so much.

"Anybody else?" One lady from the "happy to be here" group raised her hand.

"Yes."

"So, how do you like the south?" She asked in a very southern tone.

Christina gives a nervous smile. She knew she has been upset about moving to the south ever since she got here, but don't want it to be known. She chose her words wisely and said:

"It's different, but..."

"What's different?" the hoody girl interrupted.

"Now Kelsey, don't be rude," Amy scolds.

"No, it's fine," Christina defended. "It's different the atmosphere, the food..."

"What's wrong with the food?" Kelsey interrupted again. Amy glared at Kelsey and placed her index finger on her lips in a gesture to tell her to be quiet. Kelsey rolled her eyes in disregard of the gesture.

Christina grins and continues, "Nothing is wrong with it, the food is great, and it's my first-time experiencing grits in a fast-food restaurant." Everyone giggles except Kelsey.

"Different is not a bad thing. I'm enjoying it here so far."

"Well, let's begin the session," Amy said. Christina slowly took her seat. Kelsey glares at Christina. Her cold stares begin to make Christina uncomfortable. ***She's going to be an interesting case,*** Christina thought, then directs her attention to Amy and listens to the session.

When Christina got home, she rushed right into the kitchen and saw Torres sitting at the center aisle. She goes straight to the cabinet and grabs a bottle of wine.

"So, how was your day?" Christina asked while she was pouring a glass of Merlot.

"As I said before, same ole, same ole," Torres responded while checking a text message from Josh. "`Dnt 4get my Future CD tomorrow,`" it read.

"How was your day, baby?" He looked up and noticed her drinking.

"Ugh, my day was terrible, the first day on the job, and one girl already hates me."

"Who cares…OW, my shoulder is still killing me." Torres answered, wincing through the pain of his shoulder.

"I CARE, my goal is to help change lives, how am I going to do it if you don't even like me. Maybe I came on too strong or..."

"No, don't start blaming yourself," he interrupted. You can't make friends with everybody. Besides, imagine the hell I went through trying to work with a pulled muscle. I think it got worse."

"Babe, I don't even understand why you…I don't even have a response to that."

"What you mean?" Torres questioned.

She sighs and takes a drink.

"Never mind."

She sits and tries to come up with ways to gain Kelsey's trust so she can reach out to her, but her thoughts are interrupted by a knock on the door.

"Who can that be?" She looked over at Torres.

"I don't know." Torres gets up to answer it. At the door was Agali in a great mood. "Hello again," he greeted.

"Hi, um, Agali, right?" Torres asked, surprised to see him.

"That's right, sorry to come over and bother you, but I realized I didn't give you and your beautiful wife a proper welcome."

Christina walks to the door.

"Oh hi, Agali, what brings you by?"

"Hello." Agali bows to her as if she is a queen. Christina smiles. Torres had an impatient expression on his face. "Would you like to come in?" she asked.

"Thank you."

"You want a beer, man," Torres asked, trying to be polite.

"No, thank you. My visit is going to be quick. I just came to invite you and your lovely wife to my house for dinner tomorrow night."

"Oh, um…" Torres began, but Christina quickly answered.

"We would love to."

"Great! I will see you both there at six." Agali said smiling ear to ear.

"Okay, see you then, goodnight," Christina said to Agali as she walked him to the door.

"Goodnight, you all," Agali leaves with a sinister look on his face, so filled with joy, he could dance.

"Why did you say yes to that?" Torres begins as soon as the door closed.

"Because baby, that's what it means to be nice. The man came over to ask if he can make us dinner. The least we can do is go and eat it."

"No, the "least" we can do is not go at all."

Christina rolled her eyes at his comment. "Torres, it is no big deal; I mean, it's not like we had plans."

"You don't know that; I could have had plans."

"Well, do you?" Torres glares at her. "No," he answered irritably.

Christina laughs. "The best part about it is I don't have to cook."

"You do if what he cooks is some weird foreign food."

"If so, we'll order a pizza."

"You think you're funny, don't you?" He asked, but she didn't answer. She goes and pours herself another glass of wine. Torres runs behind her.

"STOP!" she squealed, "Before I spill my drink."

Torres ignores her, takes the glass from her, and drinks it down, then playfully chases Christina up the stairs.

Chapter Seven

Paul walked down the church's hallway that leads to the pastor's office, the men's and lady's restroom, and a room they called the "broom closet."

The "broom closet," a name that's recognized in many different ways, depends on who you ask. In pagan beliefs coming out of the "broom closet" meant being involved in witchery, but to Paul, the "broom closet" was literally the place they kept the broom and other cleaning supplies, or equipment. Also known as the utility room. There is where he retrieved their Hoover. He tilted the vacuum cleaner on its wheels and rolled it to the pulpit. He planned to start from the front and work his way back. As he began, the roaring sound the vacuum cleaner made caused him to miss the man slowly making his way through the church doors. Paul saw movement out the corner of his eye; that's when he looked up and saw the man staggering in. Paul notices how slowly he saunters and clutches his abdomen. Paul turns off the Hoover and watches the man as he enters. He appears to be having bad stomach pains by the way he walked, in a bent position. His eyes are watery and have bags underneath them. He looks exhausted as if it is taking all his strength to move his legs. His skin was dark brown; he wore a dingy white t-shirt and a pair of grey sweatpants. His skin sagged on his face and arms; he looked as if he lost a substantial amount of weight. "Excuse me," the man utters.

"Yes," Paul answers.

"Is the pastor here this morning?" His voice was raspy and weak. He took sharp breaths like he was having trouble breathing.

"Yes, he's in his office down the hall."

Paul came down off the pulpit to help the man to Pastor Henry's office. Paul allowed the man to lean his weight on him while he supported him. As they walked through the hallway, the man looked up and took notice of the same paintings Torres saw the day before. The portraits with biblical images reflecting famous stories from the bible. There was one painting that stood out the most to the man, but the one that caught his attention was different from the one that struck Torres. The one that fascinated the man was the story about the woman with the issue of blood. The painter illustrated a crowd of people. In the center of them all, was a man meant to be the son of God. Amid the crowd on her knees behind him, gripping the hymn of his garment was the woman. The man stared at the painting, remembering the story. He concentrated on it so, that for a moment, he stopped walking and took time to reflect on what he saw. Paul realized the man stopped walking and just thought he needed a break. He gently tugged him and encouraged him to keep going.

"We're almost there," Paul said. They continued, and Paul entered without knocking.

"What's wrong," asked Pastor Henry.

"This man is seeking your help," Paul said as he helped the man to the chair against the wall and gently seats him and leaves him with Pastor Henry.

"Hello…" the man began, out of breath from walking from the church front door to the office. "My…name… is Joseph."

"Hello Joseph, what's wrong?" Pastor Henry inquired. He got up from his desk and grabbed another folded chair that was resting against the wall and use to sit directly in front of Joseph.

"I'm in pain, Pastor" … he swallowed hard…finally able to catch his breath, he begins to tell Pastor Henry his story.

"A pain I have been dealing with for over a year. I didn't know what was wrong, I figured it was just an ulcer, I took some anti-acids and watched what I ate, it will heal itself over time, so I thought." He paused to take a few breathes to try to ease the pain he was contracting.

"You should see a doctor," advised Pastor Henry.

"Yes, when the pain started getting worst, I did seek medical attention, and the doctor told me it was stomach cancer."

"Oh, my Lord, I'm so sorry to hear that." Pastor Henry was full of remorse for the man.

"Since I waited so long, it had gotten to an advanced stage. The doctor told me chemotherapy could help prolong my life, but not…"

He stops and starts coughing uncontrollably; he reaches in his pocket for his handkerchief and covers his mouth. As he continues coughing, Pastor Henry watched as his handkerchief stains with blood.

"Are you alright, should I call for help?" Pastor Henry reached for his cell phone that was lying on his desk.

"No, that's okay." Joseph held his hand up in a gesture to say stop. Joseph controlled his coughing and continued with his story. "As I was saying, it could help prolong my life for a few more months, maybe a year, but there's no cure at this stage. I came for prayer."

Joseph answered weakly. Pastor Henry paused for a minute. He wondered why this man wasn't in a hospital. ***He has cancer***. He nodded his head yes and took Joseph's hands and began to pray. Pastor Henry prays over Joseph for about five minutes, and together they said, "Amen."

"You know there is nothing wrong with seeing another doctor for a second opinion. There are other medications besides chemo. You shouldn't give up hope on your health, seek another physician. It doesn't make you any less of a believer to seek medical help," said, Pastor Henry.

Joseph thought that was an odd thing for a pastor to say, especially after prayer. As if praying had been a waste of time, and seeking prayer was not a sign of giving up hope. Joseph felt doctors could no longer help him and that if God can't heal him, then no one can. Coming to church, he undoubtedly thought he would find somebody like-minded as he was in his beliefs, but with Pastor Henry's reaction to his problem, Joseph found he was mistaken. Joseph never responded to him; he just gave Pastor Henry a slight smile and managed to stand on his feet. Pastor Henry stood to help him out, but Joseph kindly waved him away and assured he could make it on his own.

On his way out the door, Paul rushes up to him when he saw Joseph limping out the same as he had entered.

"Are you alright," he asked.

Joseph turns and comes back in to answer him. "I'm having bad stomach pains," he replied.

"What is your name?" Paul asked.

"I'm Joseph, what's yours?"

"I'm Paul, what kind of pains are you experiencing if you don't mind me asking."

"I have cancer," Joseph sighs. It was like saying it out loud made him feel worse. "I came to the pastor for prayer, and now, I'm just waiting on Pastor Henry's prayer to work," he continued.

"That's not really how it works; it is your faith that heals you. You can pray yourself well when you believe in God's word. Do you believe Jesus is a healer?"

"Yeah," Joseph's response had no confidence in it. Pastor Henry's words had started to seep in.

"Honestly, do you believe with all your heart?"

"Yes, I do believe in God, but maybe I should seek another doctor, maybe there are other treatments…"

"Then why did you come." Paul interrupted shaking his head with disappointment.

"What do you mean?" Joseph wondered, baffled by Paul's question.

"I mean, truthfully, you didn't have to come to church to get a healing. Your God is everywhere and will not hide himself from you, knowing you are seeking him. You say you believe in God, but you don't believe you can be healed. It is insulting to God not to have faith. I thought you came here expecting a miracle, but to me, it sounds like you already accepted defeat."

"I haven't, I do believe." Joseph proclaimed.

Paul walked away and went back to the "broom closet" and grabbed a bottle of Bertolli olive oil and went back over to Joseph.

"Then pray with me."

Paul lifted his hands and then lost sight of everything; the joy in heart began to show, and praises cry out. He shouted thanksgiving then started speaking in unknown tongues. As Paul was worshiping, Pastor Henry could hear Paul's praises and shouting and comes out of his office. He walked down the hallway and saw Paul and Joseph standing five feet away from the entrance he wondered why Joseph was still there, but he didn't say anything he just stood there and watched. Paul stood there with his eyes closed, head down, and both hands rose with one of his palms facing towards the ceiling, and his other still gripping the olive oil. Joseph stands there and watches as Paul gives praise, then Joseph starts clapping his hands so he could join in the praise.

Paul calms himself and pours some of the oil in his hand and places the bottle on the floor. He rubs his hands together then puts them on, Joseph. One hand on Joseph's head and the other on Joseph's stomach, and Paul begins to pray. Paul released him and said,

"In the name of Jesus, Amen."

Paul saw Pastor Henry. He was standing there, puzzled. Paul was getting ready to ask him what was wrong, but before Paul could ask, Joseph interrupted him when he notices that he was standing upright. Joseph had received immediate healing.

"The pain is gone!" He cried out. "You truly are a man of God!" Without thinking, Joseph grabs Paul, giving him a huge bear hug.

Paul accepted his embrace. They separated, and Joseph walks out the church with his hands lifted in the air over his head, shouting praises to God. Paul stands in the doorway to wave Joseph goodbye.

"HALLELUJAH, I'M HEALED! GLORY, GLORY!" He turns and looks at Paul one last time and yells. "You have the gift of healing!"

Paul smiled and turned to go back to finish cleaning, but when he got up on the pulpit, he couldn't help that he was feeling good too and again shouted praises. Pastor Henry stood in the empty hallway filled with astonishment and some disappointment.

Chapter Eight

While Agali prepares for his dinner party, he decides to give the witch a call. “Hello,” she answered.

“I completed the spell, and I have the plan set. They will be here tonight, and I want you to be here as well.”

“NO, I agreed I would give you the spell and supplies, but I do not want part in anything else,” she spoke with authority.

“Oh, I am sorry, but you have mistaken me,” Agali responded as calmly as he could. “That was not a request. I’m telling you to be here tonight. Now, do you understand?”

She pauses for a minute, “Yes.”

“Good, I told them to come at six so you be here at five-thirty, it’s ten minutes to five, so I suggest you start getting ready now and you better be here on time.”

His words were sharp and cold. The witch had no choice but to be obedient. She felt helpless and remorseful for giving Agali the spell in the beginning. Now an innocent man is going to suffer greatly for it. The thought of that caused a pain in her stomach. She felt as if she was going to vomit. Even though she knows she is no stranger to witchcraft, the witch had to admit she has never used it in the form of jealousy but only out of revenge. She long thought of ways to get even with Agali, but her fear of him always overpowers her hate for him. Like a child following the orders of its parent, she quickly gets dressed and heads over to his house.

Agali started the food and began doing some last-minute cleaning. He runs upstairs to get the cement spreader tool from the sack the witch had given him. As he was coming back down the stairs, he hears a knock at the door. He goes to open it, not even looking through the peephole to see who it could be because he already knew. It was the witch, standing there with a depressed look on her face. Agali looks down at his watch,

"Five-twenty-five, you made it just in time, come I want to show you something."

She slowly makes her way in and closes the door behind her. She follows him into the kitchen, there he grabs the stone bowl with the mixture of dirt and blood inside and carries it into the dining room. In the dining room, around a corner in a small space was a large china cabinet. It was a dark coffee-colored brown and made of solid birch wood with beveled glass.

"Here is where I will lure Torres," he said. "This is my plan; you see these serving trays."

Agali points at a set of three silver trays stacked on top of each other, descending from small to large. They were sitting on the bottom shelf behind a glass door in the old china cabinet.

"Yes, I see them," she unhappily answered.

"I will ask him to get these trays from here and bring them into the kitchen; I'm going to spread the dirt here."

She looked at Agali and noticed he was smiling from ear to ear. He was sure he had a foolproof plan. He squats down in front of the cabinet and pulls a small round rug aside, and begins spreading a thick layer on the floor, making sure he uses as much as the mixture he could scoop out of the bowl. He uses the wooden spoon he had during the spell and the cement spreader tool. He is trying very carefully not to get any the dirt and blood mixture on himself. When he finishes, he places the rug on top of it. Agali orders the woman to watch the food while he goes outside to hose off the bowl, spoon, and the tool.

"Babe, are you ready,"

Christina asked Torres as she walks into the living room. He is sitting on the sofa playing Call of Duty on his Xbox One. Christina felt she should wear her black and white animal print summer dress for the occasion. Even though she wasn't looking forward to this dinner with Agali, she at least wanted to look as if she was excited about spending the evening with him rather than wearing an old pair of sweatpants and a bleached stained shirt. She was trying to avoid giving off that "I don't care, let's get this over with" vibe.

"Yeah, I'm ready, but damn babe, you act like we're going out or something. We're just going next door," Torres responded. He was wearing a grey t-shirt with the "Air Force" logo on it, and blue jeans.

"Please be nice, honey, at least for me."

"Whatchu mean, I'm always nice."

Christina gave Torres an "are you serious" look then rolled her eyes, dismissing that comment. Torres grinned at her expression,

"Ok, I will, baby, don't worry."

"Thank you, can you turn that game off and let's go; it's ten minutes to six."

Torres gave an exaggerated sigh... "Ok."

As they walk out the door, Agali watches them out the kitchen window. "They are on their way over, come on," Agali said to the witch. As soon as they reach his front door, Agali opens the door widely and puts a big grin on his face.

"Hello, and thanks for coming," he greeted.

"Thank you for having us," answered Christina.

"Yeah, thanks," Torres mumble with sarcasm. Christina gives him an annoyed look.

Torres smiles back at her.

"The pleasure is all mine,"

Agali responded. He was holding his hand out for Christina's. She gave him her hand, and Agali takes it and kisses it.

"So, what's for dinner?"

Torres quickly asked, displeased with Agali kissing Christina's hand. Torres wasn't oblivious of Agali's behavior, it was apparent he had a crush on Christina, and he had no problem showing it. Torres shook his head as he starts to remember how this behavior was familiar with his and Christina's relationship. They always come across people who disapprove of their interracial relationship and Agali was just like them. Torres grabbed her hand, the one Agali kissed, and laced his fingers with hers. To show Agali, Christina belonged to him. Christina gave an awkward smile when she notices the slight tension between the two. Agali just smiled. He knew in his mind that soon Torres wasn't going to be around much longer, and Agali was more than confident that soon enough, Christina will be his. Agali cleared his throat and answered Torres's question.

"I'm making a favorite from my homeland, Suya, with Jollof rice, but dinner is not quite ready yet, I am still setting the table. Please follow me into the dining room."

"What the hell did he say," whispered Torres to Christina.

"Stop," she shushes him.

"I would like you both to meet my sister, Nanja."

He introduces them to the witch. She stood there quietly, knowing her and Agali were not related or even friends, but she wouldn't dare correct him, especially in front of someone.

"Nice to meet you," Christina said as she held out her hand to shake.

Nanja responds with a soft grip. Christina notices that her hand was strangely cold, even though the air condition was on. It still wasn't freezing in Agali's home.

She must get cold quickly. She thought.

"I'm Christina Sosa, and this is my husband, Torres Sosa."

"Hi," Torres said as he shakes her hand.

"Yes, Agali has told me a lot about you, nice meeting you both."

"Please have a seat," said Agali. As soon as they sat down, Agali wasted no time starting on his plan.

"Torres, could you do me a small favor," he asked.

"What?" Torres answered, unsure of what Agali wanted.

"There are serving trays in that cabinet," Agali points at the china cabinet "could you bring them to me please, while I take out some trash. I would do it myself, but I could get dinner on the table so much faster if I had a little assistance."

Torres looks at Nanja, thinking, ***why she can't help you***. Agali caught his glance and quickly said, "My sister's been on her feet all day from working at the factory; she's exhausted...please."

Christina gives Torres another *"are you serious"* look,

"Be nice and help," she whispered.

"Um sure." Torres finally responds.

"Thank you, all you have to do is bring them into the kitchen."

Torres leans over to Christina. "Why is he taking out the trash now he could have done that when we left?"

"Please, stop, you are embarrassing me," Christina whispered, she gives Nanja a nervous smile. As Torres pushes back from his seat, getting ready to stand, he quickly grabs his shoulder in pain.

"Damn, my shoulder is still sore," he said through gritted teeth. Torres grunts through his agony. He looks up and sees Nanja staring blankly with a sorrowful expression on her face as if a doctor just told her, she only had two days to live. Torres hated very much being in Agali's home. He felt an uncomfortable negative vibe. He knew this was his first and last evening dining with him.

"Baby, are you okay?" Christina asked.

"No," Torres responded.

Nanja gets up and leaves the table to go upstairs. Nanja's slow moments, depressed nature, and eerie silence made her ghost-like in a room. Christina and Torres both looked at each other then back at her as she ascends the stairs.

"I hope there are no weapons up there because she looks suicid-al, and she might take us with her," Torres joked.

"Stop, do you want me to get the trays for you?"

"Please, I would appreciate it."

Christina sucks her teeth and pushes back from her chair to stand up. She walks around the corner, and when she gets in the small space, the stench of the hidden blood and dirt hits her.

"Ugh, what is that smell?"

She looked all around and noticed everything seem to be spot-less. She also realized she didn't smell anything until she went over there. She thought maybe it was something underneath the china cabinet.

"He needs to move this and clean underneath." She said to herself.

Christina saw the three stacked silver trays on the bottom shelf of the china cabinet behind the glass door and moves closer to the cabinet to grab them. As soon as she steps on the hidden dirt, her legs buckle, and she stumbles, catching herself by grabbing onto the china cabinet. She looked up at the beveled glass and stared at her reflection. Christina felt dizzy, so she rested against the cabinet. She took her hand and rubbed it across her face; that's when she notices she was sweating. Christina closed her eyes, trying to gather herself, surprised by the unexpected feeling that just came over her. She used her thumb and index finger to massage the bridge of her nose, trying to relieve the tension she had between her eyes. Christina took a deep breath and exhale slowly, when she opened her eyes to look back at her reflection, her eyes widen at what she saw. In the reflection of the glass, Christina saw standing behind her was the beast she had been dreaming about. The bear-shaped being was standing upright on its hind legs. It drew its long claws as it tilted its head to the side to give Christina a clear view of it in the glass. Christina's heart raced, still in disbelief of what she's seeing. Its glowing red eyes glared with a very hateful look. The beast started to snarl then opens its mouth, showing its long fangs from the top and bottom rows of its teeth. A tear falls from Christina's eye as she stares at the beast, wondering if she is dreaming again or if this is happening. The creature lunges at her. Christina gasped…jumped and quickly turned around, rattling the china cabinet, but nothing was behind her. Christina looked all around her, breathing heavily, she turned back to the glass. Nothing. Then again behind her. Nothing. Christina leans on the china closet and looks around the corner over to Torres. To see if he notices her difficulties in getting the serving trays, but she saw he hadn't notice. Torres was still rubbing his shoulder and looking down at the table, analyzing the plates and silverware in front of him. He sat there in his own little world. Torres' mind was on leaving there as soon as possible and looking at the plates was a distraction. Christina wiped her face and rubbed her eyes. She took another deep breath and let it out slowly, trying to shake the unexplainable feeling that just came over her and what she just saw. Christina took one last look at the reflection, then back behind her and again saw nothing. She shook her head, snatched the cabinet door open and grabbed the trays.

Agali comes back inside from emptying the garbage, with a devilish grin on his face. He stirs the rice in the pot and turns off the stove.

"Where do you want them?"

Agali heard Christina's voice and was confused by the question.

"Where do I want what?" Agali asked.

"The serving trays," she answered.

Agali quickly turns around and sees Christina holding the serving trays. His heart dropped down to his stomach. He was sick with a mixture of being shocked and angry.

"I did not ask you; I asked your husband!" he said in an intense and unsettling tone.

"I know, but Torres hurt his shoulder, so I got them for him. What difference does it make who gets them," she asked, stunned by the attitude that Agali had.

Angry and frustrated about the mistake, he tries to be calm.

"Never mind...I'm sorry, you can put them there. I will bring dinner out shortly."

Christina stares at Agali still surprised at his behavior. She puts the trays down and returns to her seat. Agali goes into the dining room and gets Nanja, who had return from her early departure upstairs.

"Excuse us; I need your help in the kitchen."

Nanja gets up and follows him in; as soon as they are out of sight, Agali slaps her.

"You fool!" he said in a loud whisper. "You let Christina step on the dirt!"

"What are you talking about?" she mumbled, holding her jaw in pain.

"The dirt woman, on the floor in front of the china cabinet, you let her step on it!"

"I didn't know. I got up to use the restroom."

"He was supposed to get the trays only she got them instead now the curse in on her. How do I reverse it?"

"I do not know," she answered, still in shock from the slap and of what happened.

"What do you mean you don't know?" He grabs her.

"I mean, I told you before that curse was risky, but you insisted," she whimpered.

He pushes her away in time before Christina walked in.

"Is everything okay," she asked.

"Yes, everything is fine," Agali answered.

He smiles widely, and Nanja quickly removes her hand away from her jaw.

"Dinner is ready and coming now," Agali assured.

Christina turns and leaves. Agali and Nanja walk in carrying prepared plates and switches them out for the empty plates in front of their guest.

"Wow, this looks good," said Christina. The Suya was grilled beef kebabs heavily spiced, giving a strong aroma. Jollof rice had the appearance of fried rice you get from a Chinese restaurant.

Christina eagerly tries her food. Torres, on the other hand, is hesitant. Agali and Nanja step back into the kitchen to prepare their plates; at least that was their excuse.

"Why the hell does he want serving trays if they were going to make our plates?" Torres questioned after they left the room.

"Oh my Gosh, baby, just hurry up and eat so we can leave."

Christina began to get frustrated, that whole evening seems strange, and the experience she had getting the serving trays was something she wanted to forget immediately. She was at the point where it is time to go.

"I doubt I can eat this." Torres expressed his repulse for the food.

"It's not that bad," she said as she takes a big bite out of her kebab. Torres looks at her with disgust.

"What is going to happen to her," Agali asked Nanja.

"If the person doesn't get help, there is a likely possibility they will die." Nanja answered.

Agali and Nanja rejoined their guest, having conversations as if everything was just fine. Agali swallowed up his uneasiness until dinner was over.

"Dinner was great, thanks for inviting us," Christina lied. The whole evening was terrible, but again Christina's sweet nature wouldn't allow her to be rude.

"Maybe one night, you and your sister can join us as well, right, honey."

"Yeah, right," Torres reluctantly answered.

"Yes, I enjoyed having you all, have a good night."

"Good night."

Agali waved them away with a fake smile; as soon as the door closed, he turns and glares at Nanja.

"What am I going to do? I love her; I don't want anything bad to happen to her."

"The only thing I can think of is as soon as she falls ill, convince her husband to take her to see Madam Jay."

"Madam Jay? Why can't she help me now?"

"Because she needs to be one on one with the victim. She could give you something, but it would work better if Madam Jay is face to face with the victim. Unless you want to go over to their home and confessed to what happened, the only thing you can do now is to wait."

Hearing that made Agali nauseous, the last thing he wanted to do was cause harm to his future wife. He shook his head and told Nanja she could go home now. At that moment, he just wanted to be alone.

Chapter Nine

The Possession

Torres sat at the center aisle countertop drinking his coffee and surfing the web. Checking the weather and the score from last night baseball game when he hears the creaking sound from the stairs as Christina descended from them.

"Good morning,"

He spoke without looking up from his tablet. Christina walks in, grabs a glass from the cupboard and gets some water from the tap.

"Morning…" she responded in a groggy yawn.

Torres looks up at Christina and notices her moves were sluggish. Christina turns and looks at him, and that's when he sees her eyes.

"Whoa, babe, are you alright? How did you not get any sleep last night you went to bed before me?"

"What do you mean?" She asked.

"Your eyes are bloodshot, either you've been up all night, or you got the "pink eye" in both eyes."

"What?!" Christina runs to the mirror in the living room.

"It must be my allergies." She said as she examined herself in the mirror.

She stopped examining her eyes and stares blankly into the mirror as she drifts into thought, ***the continuous nightmare has stopped, at least I think it has on the fact that now I can't even remember my dreams. Did I have a dream? I don't even remember going to bed last night.***

A truck horn honks outside and brings her back to reality. Torres comes up behind Christina gripping her waist and gently turns her to face him. "Are you sure you're feeling okay?"

"Yes, I'm fine; it should clear up on its own." She smiled.

"I'm leaving, Josh's outside, I'll see you later, my love." He kisses her on the forehead.

"Okay, honey, tell Josh I said, "hey." See you later."

Torres grabs his duffle bag from off the sofa then looks back at Christina and smiles. She smiles back and waves goodbye as he walks out the door.

Christina runs upstairs into the master bathroom and grabs the eye drops out of the medicine cabinet. As she places the drops in her eyes, she feels a cold chill. Christina shivers as goosebumps cover her arms. She takes a deep breath, as she exhales, Christina is immediately alarmed to see a breath cloud escape her mouth. Christina heart races, as panic sets in at the sudden drop in temperature. She rubs her arms to try to warm herself. ***The air conditioner is not on.***

Even if it were, it wouldn't be that cold in here. Christina stopped rubbing her arms and stood still for a moment. She felt a presence behind her. Christina could feel someone breathing on the back of her neck. She turned around quickly but saw nothing. Christina looked all around the bathroom, then stepped out into the bedroom and looked but didn't see anything. Besides, if there were someone behind her, surely, she would have heard it leave. She couldn't shake what she just felt but also couldn't explain it. ***I know I felt someone behind me. A ghost maybe. No, impossible.*** She let out a frustrated sigh and shook her head at the ridiculous thought that her house might be haunted. She went back into the bathroom and faced the bathroom mirror. Even after putting the eye drops in her eyes, there was no change. Her eyes were still red.

Christina reached down to turn the faucet on in her attempt to finish getting ready. After the water drenches her washcloth, Christina turns off the faucet. Now the only sound heard in the home, was the sound of Christina's breathing and the splashing of the water hitting the sink as she wrung out her washcloth. When Christina puts the washcloth to face to wipe the dried mucus from the corners of her eyes, a low snarl groaned in her right ear. Christina jumps then quickly turns around, looking both left and right to try to find the source of the sound, yet again, her search has come up empty. Christina could still see she's alone in the bathroom. Christina's anxiety grew worse, so to calm herself, she rushes out the bathroom to retrieve her phone charging on the nightstand. She sits on the side of the bed and calls her husband.

"Hello," he answers.

"Hey, babe um..."

Torres could hear Christina's heavy breathing. "What's wrong?" he asked.

"Nothing..."

She moves the phone away from her face for a second to steady her breathing because she didn't want to worry Torres.

"I mean, I'm not feeling well after all, my stomach's bothering me." She lied.

"Maybe it was that African food, my stomach's been bothering me too."

Christina didn't respond to Torres' comment right away. She took time enjoying the moment, Christina loves the sound of Torres's deep voice, and hearing it right next to her ear was even more soothing. She listens to him, complaining about the food and Agali without interrupting. Christina giggled a bit at some of Torres' remarks. Her smile soon fades when she notices the large black figure out the corner of her eye—standing there by the foot of the bed. Christina immediately turns her sight to where the figure stood. However, as soon as she turned her gaze in its direction, it disappeared. She shook her head in disbelief. Her educated mind refused to let her think that whatever was going on could not be explained.

"Hello...babe, you still there?"

Torres asked after Christina's long pause. Christina snaps out of her thought.

"You know what baby, you're probably right; I'm tripping. I'm going to grab some Benadryl and some ginger ale before the therapy session."

"Yeah, I told you we should not have had dinner over there. Anyway, I'll see you later, my love. You sure you're okay?"

"Yes, I'm fine. I'm sorry. I love you."

"No, don't be sorry, you know you can call me anytime. I love you too. Bye."

"Bye."

Christina takes a deep breath and exhales again; this time, she didn't see any breath cloud. "Ugh, I'm losing my mind!"

She walks back into the bathroom to continue getting ready for her day. As she walked past the mirror, she noticed even as time passed her eyes did not seem to be getting any better.

"Ah, I got to hurry up and go to the drug store; can't go to the therapy session looking like a drunk."

After showering and getting dressed, Christina spent ten minutes running up and down the stairs, retrieving forgotten items. She was in such a rush to leave that first she forgot her phone, then the keys and Christina had to run upstairs one more time to grab the notebook she uses to take notes. Christina finally gathered everything she needed and headed towards the door. She took one last look at herself in the living room mirror. She had on a white knee-length sleeveless full shoulder coverage midi dress with her black Steve Madden high heels. Her hair hangs nicely. Christina ran her fingers through it and gave it a flip and used her fingers to swoop her bang into place. She was picture perfect; the only flaw was her red eyes. She rushed out the door onto the porch but stopped when she saw Agali standing by her car. He looked worried and distracted. He wanted to talk to her to see how she was doing and find out if she was starting to feel sick so he would know how soon he should contact Madam Jay.

"What are you doing?" she asked him.

"Hello Christina.... have you been crying," he asked when he noticed her eyes.

"No, I'm fine. Why are you standing beside my car?" she asked. She instantly grew angry.

"I wanted to talk to you, I..."

"You could have knocked on the door...Christina interrupted.

THERE'S NO REASON FOR YOU TO BE STANDING ON MY PROPERTY!" she yelled.

Without thinking, Christina slaps him, causing Agali to stumble, but he was able to catch himself on Christina's car. Agali was in complete shock that such a small person could have such a powerful hit.

"I apologize; I didn't mean to upset you," Agali said with remorse.

Christina takes a moment to try to understand the situation. Christina was more than upset. She was livid. She wanted to attack Agali but didn't know why she was so angry. Christina had never been a violent person before; she realizes what she has done and begins feeling remorseful for her actions.

"I am so sorry; I don't even know why I did that." She said on the verge of tears.

"No, it's okay, I'm alright, but are you okay?"

"Um, uh…I have to go," Christina rushes past him and gets in the car.

"But wait, I need to talk to you!" Agali called out.

"I can't, I'm sorry!" Christina quickly backs out the driveway and speeds away.

Christina goes to the first drug store she comes across, and she power walks in, distraught, and in her own world. In her rush, she almost clashes into another customer. Christina continues without stopping or apologizing. She also ignores the "how rude" expression the customer had on her face, she bypasses the drugstore employee, not acknowledging his greeting or his offer for assistance. The only thing on her mind at that moment was Benadryl. As if that medication was the answer to her problems. She has forgotten all about the ginger ale even though her stomach was a little upset. All she could focus on was her eyes. She didn't want to get into a long discussion with Amy about why her eyes were red. So, she needs to clear them up fast. She reaches the area where all the different over the counter medicines were. The aisles were full of ointments, aspirins, Ibuprofen, and other medications. She came across a wall of remedies divided into three sections one labeled "cold and flu," the other "sinus and nasal, and on end was a section for "allergy" medications. Christina frantically looked on each shelf of the allergy section until she came across a square pink box of Benadryl, and quickly walks to the front of the store to get checked out.

"How are you doing today, ma'am?" asked the cashier.

A middle-aged Caucasian woman, who had the same upbeat attitude as Amy, but her appearance would remind you of a younger Carol Burnett.

"Um, fine," Christina muttered.

"Did you find everything, okay?"

"Huh…oh yeah."

"That will be six dollars and nineteen cents." Christina fumbles with her purse, she pulls out her wallet and removes her debit card.

"Is that debit or credit?"

"Huh, what?"

Christina was getting annoyed, her patience was getting short, and she was ready to leave the store, she quickly got tired of all the questions the cashier was asking her.

"Debit or credit?" The cashier asked again in a pleasant tone.

"DEBIT!" Christina snapped.

She was in a foul mood, feeling the same anger she felt with Agali. Just the sound of the cashier's voice filled her with the same rage she had for Agali. The cashier placed the pills and receipt in the bag then hands it to her. Christina snatches it from her and hurries out the door. The cashier shook her head, brushed off the rudeness, and politely greeted the next customer.

Christina hops in the Escalade, pulls down the vanity mirror, and checks her eyes to see if they were still red before she takes the pills. And to her surprise, they still were, and instead of getting better, they looked as if the red in her eyes was getting darker. She rips open the box of pills and pops two pills in her mouth and swallows hard, trying to get the dry pills down. After forcing the pills down her throat, is when she notices she forgot the ginger ale, but Christina refused to go back to the store. She had no patience at all now to deal with anybody right then. Christina huffs and begins reading the Benadryl package. She comes across the reliefs and saw that it relieves itchy, watery eyes then realized her eyes didn't itch, nor were they watery.

Christina also noticed that she didn't have any of the other symptoms listed. There was no nasal congestion, sneezing, her eyelids weren't swollen, nor were her eyes sensitive to light. She didn't have any trouble seeing. The only problem she had was the discoloration other than that there was no discomfort. She then grasped the thought that her red eyes were not the result of an allergic reaction. ***Maybe Torres was right. Perhaps I am getting "pink eye," and the irritation hasn't started yet.*** Christina again tries to come up with a logical reason to make herself feel better. She looked through her purse to find her eye drops and added another dose to each eye. She glanced at her watch and saw it was 8:45 am, and her session was at 9:00 am.

"Shit, I need to go now; I'm going to be late."

She tosses the drops and pills in her purse, cranks up, and speeds off. She reaches a green traffic light, but it changes to yellow, she was going to continue through, but the car in front of her slows down and stops as the light changes to red. Christina had to slam on brakes to prevent from hitting the car in the back.

"DAMN IT. You could have made that!"

She shakes her head in aggravation and sighs in frustration. When she inhaled, she notices a filthy smell filled the air. She takes quick breaths, sniffing the air trying to figure out what caused the smell. She knows the car is spotless, Torres takes a lot of time in vacuuming and spraying fabric refresher on the carpet, and not to mention the black ice scented tree hanging on the rearview mirror. Still, the putrid odor masked all the fresh scent dispersed throughout the car.

"I must have passed some roadkill or something."

She said as she rolled up the windows. The light changes to green, and she quickly maneuvers into the next lane and passes the car that slowed her down, in a hurry to make it to the session in time.

Chapter Ten

Paul struggled to get the box of church fans out of the back seat of his navy blue 1995 Chevrolet Monte Carlo.

"How did he get this in here," He thought out loud.

The "he" Paul was referring to was his fellow church member and roommate, who ordered the fans for the church. He left to visit family and before leaving asked if Paul would deliver them to the church. Paul takes his passenger seat, grips the level underneath, and pulls it as far up as it could go. Then he manages to squeeze the box out of the gap he created. Paul cradles the box in one arm, walks up the steps and unlocks the church's door. Tonight, is Wednesday night bible study, and he wants to get the church ready. He drops the box at the start of the pews and grabs two hands full of fans, then walks down each aisle of the pews and places four fans in the pocket on the back of each set of seats. Making sure everyone can get one. While he was placing the fans, Pastor Henry walks in. Paul heard the heavy door open and close. He turns around to see who had entered.

“Hello Pastor, how are you doing today, Paul greeted as Pastor Henry came in.

“I’m good, thank you, how about yourself.”

“I’m great, happy to live another day serving the Lord,” Paul answered, smiling ear to ear.

Pastor Henry gave a slight smile back.

“Life’s perfect, huh?” Pastor Henry asked rhetorically, thinking he already knew the answer.

“No, not at all, I have problems like everyone else, like now I’m trying to find a job,” Paul responded.

“What happened to your warehouse job?” Pastor Henry asked, surprised that Paul’s mood didn’t match what he was going through.

“I was laid off.” Paul shrugged as his way of saying, “it happens.” “There’s nothing I can do about it.”

“Weren’t you there for a while?”

“Yeah, I was, but I was also just a temp. The temp agency said they would find me another position somewhere else, so I’m not worried.” Paul smiled.

“Why are you in such a great mood?” Pastor Henry wondered.

“I’m lit up from the healing Joseph received the other day!”

Paul grinned, he was genuinely happy for Joseph and loved seeing the incredible blessings God does; it strengthens his faith. “I know if God did it for one, he would do it for all. Besides, you know the bible tells us to be thankful in all situations. It says, “In every thing give thanks: for this is the will of God in Christ Jesus concerning you.” (1 Thessalonians 5:18 KJV)

“Yeah…Joseph,”

Pastor Henry replied, completely ignoring the scripture Paul quoted. In Pastor Henry's heart, he knows it to be true, but it's hard to live that way. To be thankful even in a moment of loss or great disappointment is easier said than done. Pastor Henry shook his head and started walking towards his office.

"May I ask, what are you teaching tonight?" Paul questioned.

"I'm sorry?" Pastor Henry was in such a hurry to go to his office; he missed Paul's question.

"Tonight, at service, what book are you teaching from?"

"Oh, I haven't decided yet, and I'm going to my office to work on that now."

"You didn't pray about it," Paul asked.

"Um, I'm going to do that now." Pastor Henry quickly responded.

"Any book God gives you to teach would be good. I hope tonight or sometime soon though it will be something from Hebrews."

"Why, Hebrews?" Pastor Henry inquired.

"A scripture came to me last night, in a dream, Hebrews eleven and six. "But without faith it is impossible to please him: for he that cometh to God must believe that he is, and that he is a rewarder of them that diligently seek him," (KJV) "You know, saints need to learn more about faith so when things don't go the way they thought it would, they won't be discouraged. How will they know about faith if no one teaches it," Paul continues quoting another scripture, "So then faith cometh by hearing, and hearing by the word of God." (Roman 10:17 KJV)

Paul's words struck Pastor Henry like a falling brick.

"Well, who knows, the answer might be Hebrew since you dreamt it." Pastor Henry answered.

"Maybe,"

Paul shrugged again this time to say he did not know. Paul

had a lot of faith. Going to church to him was like a second home. Even though he has read the bible from cover to cover, he is not arrogant, to be a "know it all" about the bible and how a person should live his or her life. He is not one to judge, not just because the scriptures speak against it, but he's just not that type of person. He knows if it weren't for grace, we all would be in trouble, including himself. He does ministers to people who seek advice from him. Sometimes he wonders could he be a pastor at his own church, but the idea of having his church is not so big that he is not humble enough to serve in someone else's. He figures if he is serving the Lord and doing it from a place of love. Then he's okay with that. Paul does admire Pastor Henry, but he notices Pastor Henry sometimes has a depressing nature. Even though he doesn't show it often, Paul can still discern that something is wrong, and that Pastor Henry is going through a personal storm. He prays for him every night that the Lord will strengthen his heart.

Pastor Henry sits at his desk groaning and stares out in the open. He is deeply depressed and thinks he is doing an excellent job of hiding it. Pastor Henry doesn't know that Paul suspects something is wrong. He couldn't stop thinking about Joseph, and how he came for his help, and Pastor Henry let him down, just like he let his father down two years ago. Pastor Henry stares at the empty chair in front of his desk as his mind flashes back to that night:

"The nurse said his room is down this way," Pastor Henry said to his family as he leads the way down the hospital halls. He opened the room door and allowed everyone to enter, making him the last to go in. Pastor Henry, his wife Elisabeth, his older brother William, or Billy, is what the family calls him. Along with his wife Evelyn and their mother, Helen, all surrounded his dying father, William Henry Sr. His father has prostate cancer. He laid there, barely moving. He

would only maneuver his head from side to side, looking at his family. The room was silent; the only sounds were the beeping from the monitor and the footsteps in the hallway from passing nurses. Pastor Henry broke the silence with a question to his father. "Hey pa, you are feeling any better?" He gently caresses his father's head. "No, son...I feel the same." He utters. "It's going to be ok," Pastor Henry assured. "Yeah, pa, you know you're tough as a bull if anybody can beat this, you can," Billy added. The doctor knocked, then entered the room; he was carrying William Sr's test results. The doctor read from his chart notes and shook his head. He requests for Helen, William Sr.'s wife to join him outside the room so he could break the news to her privately. Hellen refused, she assured the doctor that whatever he needed to tell her, he could say it in front of the entire family. So, the doctor begins, "He has maybe a few more days," he said. Pastor Henry's mother burst into tears, heartbroken over the horrible news. Elisabeth wraps her arms around the grieving soon to be a widow to console her. Pastor Henry refused to accept that diagnosis. He walked over to the doctor and looked him directly in the eyes. "I know you think you have it all figured out, and sir, I'm sure you are a brilliant man, and you are only giving your medical opinion, but I have seen God work when science had failed." The doctor kindly rested his hand on Pastor Henry's shoulder and said, "I know this is hard to hear, and I'm so sorry, but your father might not make it through the night." Pastor Henry looked around at his family, then back at the doctor. "Please, leave." He requested. As soon as the doctor walked out of the room, Pastor Henry closed the door behind him. He asked the family to gather around the bed and get down on their knees to pray. They did, and they all prayed together.

"We had faith..." Pastor Henry spoke out loud at his desk.

His flash from the past is causing him to relive that moment.

"I believe in miracles…What happen?"

The next morning after Pastor Henry told the doctor he was wrong. His father went into cardiac arrest and later died. It was that day when Pastor Henry began to lose his faith. He never mentioned how he felt to anyone but, ever since that day, he has been discouraged. Pastor Henry heard a thud in the church, Paul accidentally dropped one of the collection plates, and the sound knocked him out of that memory. He sighs…opens his bible and starts skimming through Hebrews.

Chapter Eleven

Christina reaches the help center two minutes before it was time for the therapy session to begin. Luckily, there were a couple of ladies from the group just getting there themselves. Amy stood in the doorway, holding the door open for the guest and talks to some of them as they entered in. Christina rubs her stomach; she was getting this nauseating feeling and her heart begins to race. She feels like she's having an anxiety attack. Christina tries to shake it off as she quickly gathers her things, her breathing quickens, and dizziness hits her hard like the car was just lifted in a tornado and placed back on the ground.

Damn what was in that food, I've never felt like this before. Christina thought as she tries to relax her breathing. She took a deep breath then exhaled when she attempted to take another deep breath, the awful smell assaults her nose again,

"WHAT IS THAT!" she exclaimed, wrinkling her nose.

Then, a low growl emerges from behind her. It was like an angry wolf was sitting in the back seat of the car. She looks back and around but doesn't see anything.

"Okay, relax, get these four hours over with then go home and go straight to bed."

She said as she coaches herself in making it through that session. Christina gets out of the car and starts walking towards Amy. She plasters a fake smile on her face and continues towards her. Christina slows down from her power walk towards Amy. She has this overwhelming feeling that someone else is watching her every move, which was unlikely since there was no one else in the parking lot. Everyone who was coming had already gone in, and Amy stood in the doorway, talking to one of the abused women while she held the door open, waiting for Christina. Then again, she hears a long and loud growl, the sound a wolf makes when it is getting ready to attack. It is so close; Christina could feel it breathing on her neck. She quickly turns around and looks, but there was nothing there. Amy looks back towards Christina, wondering what was taking her so long to walk from her car to the door. That was when she noticed Christina's sudden jerks.

"Did you forget something?"

"Huh?" Christina turned and directed her attention back on Amy.

"Did you forget something, honey?"

"Oh no, I thought I did." Christina lied.

The last thing a psychiatrist should say is, *"I'm hearing and feeling things that aren't there."* She continues, and the growls grew closer.

"Is there a dog around here?" Christina asked as she approached Amy.

"A dog?" Amy responded, puzzled by the question.

"Oh yeah, my allergies are already bothering me, and I'm very allergic to dogs."

Christina's lies continued; what she wanted to know was where those growls were coming from.

"Oh, poor thing, I see, your eyes are red, but no, not as I know of."

Christina was stunned. Amy noticed her eyes. ***I can't believe my eyes are still red after all this time and medicine I took. It should be getting better.***

"Are you okay?" Amy asked with concern.

"Yes…yes, I'm fine, let's go begin the session."

Christina followed Amy though the building, they walked down the corridor and entered a large room; this room was bigger than the previous place they all met the last time. Christina looked around and noticed there were also more abused women there than before. Instead of the eight, there were over thirty. All filled the room with the same three personalities. The "happy to be here" group, the "I don't want to be here" group, and there were three more ladies to add to the scared and paranoid section. There were a few things all these women had in common; they all came from domestic abuse shelters. They all were noticeably battered and needed counseling. Even the "happy to be here," women needed some emotional therapy. They were happy to be away from their abusers, but they battled with their low self-esteem and insecurities. The crowd of abused women sat in a half-circle in front of a podium and three chairs. The rostrum was centered, and the three chairs were behind off to the right side. In the chair farthest to the right was an older woman whose appearance would remind you of Jane Hathaway from the Beverly Hillbillies, but had the personality of Mrs. Drysdale. She was skinny as a stick and had a snobbish and proud expression covering her face. Amy and Christina approached her, and Amy began with the introduction.

"Christina, this is Dr. Linda Rogers."

"Nice to meet you,"

Christina held her hand out to shake. Dr. Rogers responded to the handshake and said,

"Yes…Christina, Ms. Simpson, gave me a brief description of you. Hmm, I see someone is already having a rough morning."

Dr. Rogers noticed Christina's eyes and naturally had to give an inappropriate comment about it. She had a snobby way about her. It was that day when Dr. Rogers learned she was not the only psychiatrist speaking. She already had her mindset to say everything and cover all aspects of the session to leave Christina speechless. There was no way she was going to let Christina outdo her. Christina ignored her; her mind couldn't focus on anything or anyone. Instead of competing with Dr. Rogers, she decided to let her do all the talking. Christina felt weak and weary. The last thing she wanted to do was get into a catfight.

"Ladies, thanks again for joining my organization, and I'm glad we all have the same goal, and that's to help these women move on in their lives."

As Amy spoke, she watched Christina. She saw how weary she looked and knew something was wrong.

"Are you sure you're okay?" Amy whispered to her.

"I'm fine," Christina quickly defended. Christina again put on a fake smile and, for a moment, made herself look like she was full of energy.

"Okay, who wants to speak first?" Amy asked.

"I do!" Dr. Rogers blurted out.

As if it was a surprise. Amy went up to the podium to introduce Dr. Rogers. Christina took a seat and exhaled her exhaustion.

"Welcome back to the familiar faces, and welcome to our newcomers we are happy to have you. I don't know about my psychiatrists, but I was once in an abusive relationship ten years ago. That's what inspired me to start this organization. I want to give the same help I received years ago.... Uh mm", she clears her throat. "Excuse me."

Amy had to pause. She was getting emotional.

"I want to introduce one of today's speakers Dr. Linda Rogers, let's all give her a warm welcome." Everybody clapped collectively while Dr. Rogers took her place at the podium.

"Hello everyone,"

She said in a charming tone like she was such a gentle and kind-hearted person. Christina rolled her eyes at Dr. Rogers's fraudulent behavior. All Christina wanted to do was take a nap, knowing that it was not possible to do now. She sat up straight and rested against the chair and her head on the wall. Christina slipped off her heels halfway. She kept her feet in her shoes because she didn't want the fact that they were off too noticeable. Though high heels are cute, they aren't the most comfortable shoes. Christina closed her eyes to rest them for a minute while she listens to Dr. Rogers's boring speech, quoting everything she got out of every book she ever read on psychology. Five minutes had passed, and Christina finds herself dozing off. The drop in her head is what woke her. She glanced over at Amy to see did she notice, but she was busy taking notes.

Christina leans her head from side to side popping her joints, trying to relax her neck. She straightens back up in her seat, makes herself alert, and listens to the session. Christina stares at the back of Dr. Rogers' head and tries to focus on the lecture she was giving. About five more minutes had passed, and the sound of Dr. Rogers' voice, everything and everyone in the room begin to fade out. Christina could only hear the growling. She slowly turns her head to look around, trying not to look frantic. Then someone or something begins to whisper incoherently. Christina's first reaction was to look to her right, to see if Amy was saying something to her, but she wasn't, Amy was focused on Dr. Rogers' speech. The whispers grew louder, but Christina could not make out what they were saying. Christina scanned the crowd to see if anyone was whispering to each other. She went down the rows and checked each person, but no one was talking except Dr. Rogers, and unbelievably, she couldn't hear her at all. Christina could see Dr. Rogers' lips moving, but no sound came out. There was no sound, excluding the occasional growls and whispers. Christina was getting nervous; sweat poured down her back. She looked around wildly, not caring who notice but could not find the source of the sounds. She stops, closes her eyes, and takes a deep breath, and exhales, trying to calm down. Then everything was silent. Her breathing steadies her nerves were calming, and she gave sigh of relief. Christina thought it was over until she heard....

"He's here." The whisper was eerie and clear. It sounded like a woman purposely making her voice childlike. The voice came from her left side; she opens her eyes and looks left. Standing there in the corner of the room is the beast. The same one she had been dreaming about for weeks, the same creature who stalked her at Agali's house, is now crouched down on all fours just ten feet beside her. Christina's first thought was maybe she fallen asleep again, and it was a dream. She closed her eyes and started pinching herself hard. The third pinch she gave herself broke the skin. Once she realized she was awake, she opens her eyes and turns to Amy to ask her a question.

"When will it be my turn to speak, she whispered."

"Soon, honey, don't worry, there'll be time for you too."

Christina didn't care about speaking to the group at that moment. She was simply happy she could hear Amy's voice. ***Okay, okay, everything's fine***, she thought. Christina let out another sigh of relief, she felt relaxed, until she started to see movement out the corner of her left eye. Christina turned her head to the left again, and to her shock, the beast was still there—Christina whimpers. She was causing all the attention in the room to be on her. Dr. Rogers grew very annoyed about the fact she was interrupted and had no sympathy for Christina even though she was upset. Amy tries calling her name, trying to get Christina's attention to see what's bothering her, but Christina could no longer hear Amy. It was like the beast's piercing glowing red eyes had her in a trance.

Amy looked past her to see what it was that had Christina's attention, but the corner Christina was staring into had nothing there. The beast looked angrier than it did in her dreams, and its rage was worse than when she saw it at Agali's house. Snarling showing its fangs, it let out a loud guttural roar. It charges toward Christina with incredible speed. It leaped in the air with its claws drawn, and mouth wide opened. Christina let out an ear-splitting scream and fell to the floor. Everyone was frightened by her. They couldn't see anything attacking her, but Christina was acting as if she was going to die. Amy fell to her knees beside Christina and grabbed her.

"CHRISTINA, CHRISTINA! WHAT'S WRONG!" Amy shouted.

Christina fought and cried. The crowd all stood to their feet and watched Christina's hysteria. Christina was now on the floor in front of Dr. Rogers. She stood there, watching in terror while Christina kicked and screamed.

"HELP! HELP, GET IT OFF ME!" Christina yelled at the top of her lungs.

Amy wrestles on the floor with Christina trying to calm her down. Amy looked up at Dr. Rogers for help controlling her. As Dr. Rogers reluctantly decides to go and help Amy, she immediately stops in her tracks when Christina throws her head back and lets out another ear-piercing scream, that's when Dr. Rogers notices her eyes glowed at that moment. Dr. Rogers backed away from them and went into the crowd. Amy, however, didn't see it; she was too busy trying to dodge Christina's kicks. The women in the group whispered and pointed.

"Is this lady supposed to be helping us, she can't even help herself."

One of them said to the other. The four paranoid women were starting to panic; their nerves could not handle this type of excitement. Christina could see and feel the beast biting into her chest. She cried out in pain as it sank its teeth into her flesh and clawed her. It was ripping her apart. She closed her eyes, unable to handle the site of it. Her throat was raw from all her screaming.

"CHRISTINA, IT'S ALRIGHT!" Amy shouted.

Christina opened her eyes when she heard Amy's voice. She saw that the beast was gone. Christina broke free from Amy's arms and managed to get on her feet. She looked around franticly, trying to see where the creature went, but there was no sign of it. Christina felt all over her body, looking for wounds and blood, but there was nothing there, no lacerations of any kind. All she had was a sore throat.

"Christina, what's wrong.... say something." Amy pleaded.

The room was silent, and all eyes were on her. Christina looked at Amy and burst into tears. There was no way she could give a logical explanation or even try to explain what happened without getting a suggestion to check into the insane asylum. Amy went towards her to try to hug her, but Christina backed away and ran out the door. Amy wanted to run after Christina. She stopped when she heard whimpering from one of the paranoid women, who was on the verge of a breakdown from all the excitement. Amy realized she needed to stay with the abused women and try to finish the session. Instead of chasing after Christina, with a heavy heart, Amy felt it would be best to stay, so she goes and consoles the paranoid woman.

It wasn't until Christina got outside when she realized she forgot her purse and all her things including the car keys but had no intention of going back in there. She also left her shoes by mistake as well, she intended to slip them back on when it was her turn to speak to the group, but never got to that point. So, Christina left her car at the center and started walking home barefoot. As she walked, she checked her body one more time to see the damage that the beast has left, but there was none. Christina just knew what she saw and felt was real but had no way to explain it. Something was wrong, and she didn't know what to do. She had a hard time forming a clear thought. It was like something else was thinking for her. She found herself blacking out but still moving. She was walking but could not see where she was going. She didn't walk into anything or anybody. It was like somebody was walking for her, and she had no control over her body. That feeling of having no power over your body was unbearable. She wanted to ask for help or, at the very least, ask someone if she could use their phone so she could call her husband, but she couldn't get her mouth to open. Christina could hear herself screaming in her head. She couldn't even stop walking if she wanted to. Christina must deal with the torture of waiting for this feeling to pass. Time had passed, and the grip that had a hold of her finally released; the blackout was over, and she could finally see where she was going, but it was then when Christina realizes she was not walking upright on two feet. She was on her hands, soles of her feet with her back arched and her head up. Christina had been walking like a four-legged animal. She stopped and dropped to her knees as she examined her hands and saw how dirty they were. They were scraped and bleeding. She glanced down at her watch. She had been walking like that for over an hour and didn't know it. She jumped to her feet and started running. Halfway down the road, she saw a church with two cars parked out front. It was Pastor Henry's church, but Christina was unaware because she had never visited. She ran towards it, hoping someone inside could help her. She thought maybe she could use their phone, or someone would be kind enough to give her a ride home.

Paul had finished getting the church ready for tonight's service. After he put the remaining fans away in the broom closet, he looked around the church to double-check that he completed all his tasks. When Paul saw, he had done everything needed to do to prepare for Wednesday night bible study. He decided to go up to the altar to pray before saying goodbye to Pastor Henry. Paul walked up to the altar and got down on his knees, bowing to his living God. As he prayed, Christina walked up the four red-bricked steps, gasping, out of breath from running. A feeling of hope came over her when she saw she was almost there.

As soon as Christina opened the door, the same creepy voice she heard earlier yelled out, "NO!"

Then a force grabs her from behind and snatches her back, sending her flying backward. She screams as she lands flat on her back on the ground, and the door slams close. Christina's scream sounded more like a wounded animal than a human. Paul, startled by the cry and the door slamming, sprang to his feet.

"Oh, my Lord," he gasped.

Paul searched the church to see what or who had entered, but there was no one there. He rushed to the door and opened it, but again no one was there. He ran outside into the road looking all around, trying to find out what happened and who was that. Paul was unaware that it was Christina because the two have never met. Even if he had known her, he still wouldn't have recognized that scream. That scream he heard reminded him of a dog yelping after you accidentally step on its paw. It maybe took Paul fifteen seconds to run from the altar to the door, and Christina was already gone. It was like she vanished just as quickly as she appeared. Pastor Henry came and stood at the top of the church steps. He saw Paul standing in the middle of the road searching all around.

"What happened, why did you slam the door?!" Pastor Henry shouted to Paul.

Paul looked directly at Pastor Henry shaking his head from side to side.

"I didn't. I didn't slam the door; I'm out here trying to figure out what did!" He responded.

Pastor Henry could hear and see the seriousness of Paul, and it made him nervous. ***What did he mean "what" slammed the door, maybe he missed spoke and meant who?*** Pastor Henry thought but decided not to ask.

Christina was staggering from fatigue. She reached a restaurant with an outdoor patio. She sat at one of the tables and whimpered, rocking back and forth. Christina felt she is a knowledgeable and coherent person, but she could not even begin to explain why she was going through this. A man at the table across from her…stared. He was a potbelly "Homer Simpson" looking guy, and quickly grew an attitude; he couldn't enjoy his food with Christina's sobbing disturbing him. Christina's eyes were now swollen and red from her uncontrollable sobbing. Christina's tears were streaming down, and snot ran from her nose. She was a mess.

The teenage waitress saw Christina sitting at one of the tables she is assigned to but felt uncomfortable to approach her. She assumed Christina was just sitting there for a second and wasn't going to order. So, the young waitress passed by Christina and waited on another table. The man stared at Christina deeply, hoping his glares would get her attention and let her know she needed to leave. Suddenly, Christina's sobbing stopped abruptly. Her head dropped down, and her arms fell by her sides. She blacked out again; she sat completely still and quiet for a moment. The fake Homer Simpson, glares turn into perplexed stares. Christina didn't move an inch, but she begins to growl and snarl. It was then when the man was convinced that Christina was crazy, as he raises his arm and moves his index finger back and forth in a "come here" gesture trying to call the young waitress over to his table so he could tell her to get the manager and make Christina leave. The young waitress saw him and nodded at him to acknowledge she saw his request and was coming. She finished taking the order of an older couple.

Then turned and headed towards the fake Homer Simpson's table. When the waitress got in three feet of him, …he burst into flames. The waitress screams and the man cried out in pain and terror, the waitress ran into the restaurant to get help, and other customers shouted and scattered from the chaos. The stench of his burning body lingered in the air. Some of the customers who were still there, gagged from the odor. Some tried to get close to the burning man and throw their glasses of water on him, but could not get close enough to him because of the smell, the scent wasn't a usual smell of burning flesh, but an aroma similar to ammonia came from the man. Even when they tossed their water anyway, it fell short, missing him or would splash back into their faces. It was like an invisible barrier was in between the man and the people trying to help. Christina stood up slowly with her head still down and arms by her sides and walked away from it all. The fire that consumed the man was so intense he melted away. The waitress alerted the manager, who called the paramedics, but it was a waste of time. The man died in a matter of minutes. There was nothing left but a pile of ashes.

Chapter Twelve

Agali knew from the experience he had that morning with Christina something was wrong. The spell was reacting in a way he didn't expect, and everything was spiraling out of control. He knew he needed to do something quick to fix it before it was too late. So, he decided to go ahead and invite Madam Jay over. He paced the floor waiting for her to arrive. He bought a pack of cigarettes to smoke because his wooden smoking pipe wasn't enough anymore. His stress level was through the roof. The one person who he wanted so badly is the one he's badly hurting. He was anxious, hoping Madam Jay will be able to help him and fast before Christina gets worse. Someone knocks at the door; he puts out his tenth cigarette of the day and rushes over to answer it. Madam Jay stood there with a serious look in her eyes. She was an old brown skin Gullah, with a small and frail body, she had long black and grey dreads and wore a long plain black dress. She stood there and stared with her lite grey eyes.

"Please, please come in," Agali pleaded.

He had great respect for the Geechee and heard Madam Jay was good at what she does. It was when he moved to South Carolina twenty years ago, is when he first heard about the Gullah people. Fascinated by them, he spent three years learning their ways and language. The Gullah people spoke creole English. Essentially, they speak English but have a unique way of doing so. It took a lot of practice, but eventually, Agali caught on to their language and now understands them very well.

Madam Jay or Ma'am Jay is what the Gullah called her, was one of many Root workers among her kind.

"One people een trubble talk'um tuh me, wuh happ'n?" [Only people in trouble talk to me, what happen] Madam Jay inquired.

Agali took her by the hand and guided her to the window. The one he and Nanja had watched out of before. To explain his reason for calling her.

"Therein that house" …he pointed to the Sosa's residence. "Is a beautiful woman that I fell madly in love with, but the problem is she's married."

"Ok," Madam Jay responded waiting on more explanation.

"See, I was willing to do whatever it takes to make her mine. So, I got a spell from a friend, an idiot, who allowed everything to go wrong."

"Wuh happ'n?" [What happen] Madam Jay asked again, she was growing impatient of Agali's rambling.

Agali sighs, "Honestly; I don't know. I conjured a spirit of jealousy to use to kill the woman I love husband, but she got the spell on her instead of it getting on him."

"Iz é nigh de't?" [Is she dying] Madam Jay asked

"I don't know, but I know something is very wrong. My friend warned me the spell was dangerous. Listen, Madam, I am willing to pay you $1,000 for your services and buy all the supplies you may need to help me."

Madam Jay's interest perked after Agali's offer. She has never made that much on a case before. She nodded her head in acknowledgment of his proposal as Agali continues.

"I can see a difference in my love than how she was before. When I first met her, she was so sweet and gentle, but this morning when I went over to talk to her, not only did she snap at me, but she also struck me."

"Oonuh call sumbody hab a bad day nut bein' demself?" [You call someone having a bad day not being themselves]

"You don't understand, it wasn't just the fact that she hit me, but the power behind the blow, she's a small woman, but she had the strength of a linebacker. I mean, it was like…"

Agali paused when he saw a car enter the Sosa's driveway. It was Amy, she came over to return Christina's purse and shoes and to see how she was doing.

"Please excuse me for one-minute, madam,"

Agali said as he pushed past her to go out of his front door. Madam Jay gave Agali an irritated look and shook her head, thinking he was all over the place. She gazed out the kitchen window and watched as Agali headed over to the Sosa's to meet Amy.

Amy knocked and rang the doorbell, but no one answered. She listened carefully to see if she could hear someone moving around in the home but heard nothing. Amy sighed in disappointment; She wanted to see Christina and was worried sick about her. When she turned to go back to her car, Amy saw a man coming towards her.

"Hello, can I help you?"

Agali asked as he approached her. Amy thought for a second;

she knew he wasn't Christina's husband because she remembered Christina saying her husband is Hispanic.

"Uh, who are you?" Amy questioned.

"I'm Agali Sawadogo; I'm a friend and neighbor to the Sosa's. They're not home right now." Agali explained.

"Okay, do you know when they will be back?"

"No, but I will be happy to give them a message."

He answered, hoping she will tell him something. He wanted to know what was going on and was Christina alright. He was also curious about who Amy was. Agali has been stalking the Sosa's home since they moved in and has never seen Amy visit there before.

"Well, um, Christina left her things, and I was trying to return it." Amy immediately grew uncomfortable with Agali's presence; she took notice when she drove up that there was no one outside, then suddenly, Agali appears a few minutes after she had parked and knocked on the Sosa's door.

"I'll give it to her." Agali reached out for Christina's things, but Amy backed away.

"That's okay. I rather give it to Christina myself."

Amy had no intention of giving Christina's items to a stranger, even if he is her neighbor. She just looked at him and gave a nervous smile.

Meanwhile, Madam Jay continued to watch out of Agali's kitchen window. She yawns as she looks up at the white circular analog clock on the wall to see what time it was, Madam Jay was tired of being there and was ready to leave, she felt Agali was overreacting and worrying about nothing. Usually, when people contact her, they are in dire need of help, but from what Agali described so far about his problem didn't relate to Madam Jay's usual cases. However, she still plans to assist him and earn the grand he is so willing to pay. She directed her attention back out the window, looking towards Agali and Amy. Agali had left his pack of cigarettes sitting on the kitchen countertop, while Madam Jay gazed out the window, the pack of cigarettes began moving on its own from side to side. Madam Jay heard the scratching sound the plastic wrapper made as it rubbed against the countertop.

Even though she listened to the noise, she didn't know what it was, and Madam Jay didn't see the cigarettes moving on its own because of the small wall that hugged the countertop blocking her view from where she was standing. So, she ignored the faint sound; the movement of the cigarettes wasn't a loud noticeable noise. The only reason she heard it is because there was no other sound in the house. Other than the ticking of the analog clock. The pack of cigarettes continues to rustle on the countertop. Suddenly the cigarettes flew off the countertop bouncing off the wall and crashing onto the floor. As if someone picked them up and threw them. That sound causes Madam Jay to leave the window and search for the source of the noise. When she comes around the wall-hugging the countertop, Madam Jay immediately saw the cigarettes on the floor. In her mind, it simply fell. She disregards it, picked up the pack of cigarettes, and placed them back on the countertop. She sighs, tired of standing there waiting on Agali. She decided to go into the living room and have a seat on the sofa, but before she went, she wanted to see was Agali on his way back. She goes to glance out the window one more time.

"Whoa!" Madam Jay let out a surprised scream.

Christina stood there pressed against the window, staring at Madam Jay with glowing blood-red eyes. Madam Jay slowly backed away from the window, closed her eyes, and started quoting the Lord's prayer in her native language. She heard a rustling sound by the window. She opened her eyes to see Christina was no longer there. Madam Jay eased over closer to the window to get a better look out of it and saw Christina was now in her yard standing right behind Agali.

Agali was about to insist that Amy could trust him with Christina's stuff, but before he was able to, he felt something behind him. He quickly turned around and saw Christina standing there motionless. Her head dropped down and arms by her sides like before when she left the restaurant. Without lifting her head, Christina spoke.

"What are you doing here?" Christina asked through gritted teeth. They both were startled when they saw her.

"Christina, honey, we need to talk," Amy begged, "There's something very wrong I know it. Is the job becoming overwhelming? Because if it is, I understand if you need to take some time off."

Christina stood silently. Agali's heart began to beat rapidly, to see Christina in the state she was in was devastating because he knew it was his fault. ***What have I done?*** He thought. Christina continued to stand still, not showing any type of acknowledgment that she heard what Amy said.

"Christina, I brought you your purse and shoes, you left it at the center,"

Amy looked down at Christina's feet and saw how dirty they were. She regretted she didn't run after Christina. Still, Amy felt obligated that she needed to stay and calm the ladies down at the therapy session then reschedule another get together with them. She was saddened to know that Christina walked all the way home. Amy held Christina's things out to her. Christina rudely pushed passed her, shoving Amy in the process. Christina had no interest in retrieving anything. Agali gave Amy a sorrowful look but said nothing. He just held out his hand to again insist Amy to let him take Christina's things for her, but Amy refused. Amy didn't want to leave Christina's things there on her porch, worried Agali would take it since he was more interested in getting it than Christina. She decided to keep Christina's things and would try again when Christina felt better. Amy ran to her car with her eyes filling with tears. Christina gave Agali an evil look. Her eyes were no longer glowing, but the same discolored red as they were this morning when he spoke to her. Christina's glares were cold. If looks could kill, Agali would be dead. He backs away and heads over to his house. Christina turns and faces to her front door, staring at it blankly, the door unlocks itself and opens, and she enters in.

Agali comes into his home with his head hung low; Madam Jay hurries over to him as soon as he closes the door.

"Uh see um!" [I saw her] She exclaimed. "Wuh do' oonuh duh?" [What did you do?] That question pierced Agali's heart.

"Can you help me?" he uttered.

"Uh kin, dey iz uh ritual uh kin duh, dat could rid um uh ebil sperrits, but uh need tuh be nigh um." [I can, there is a ritual I can do that could rid her of evil spirits, but I need to be near her.]

"Madam, that's impossible, how are we going to convince her husband to agree to let us see her?"

Agali's worry was making him sick. Everything was out of control. One mistake ruins his chance for a wife. He never acknowledges the fact that he destroyed an innocent couple's lives. His selfishness only leads him to self-pity. He could care less about Torres; besides, he was trying to kill him anyway.

"Don' worry," [Don't worry] Madam Jay began, she walks over to the sofa and sits down. "W'en um husband see um, é will be baiging fuh help." [When her husband sees her, he will be begging for help] Agali gave no response, he just sits on the sofa beside her.

Chapter Thirteen

Paul entered his home, dragging his feet, exhausted, after a long day. He rented a room from a retired Navy veteran. He was Senior Chief Petty Officer Justin Tangredi, a title he wore proudly. Tangredi was currently out of town for two weeks visiting his daughter. It was the last two weeks before school started, and he wanted to spend time with his grandchildren before they went back to school. Paul was enjoying having the house to himself, although he got along with Mr. Tangredi very well; there is nothing like having your own home. No roommates, no asking permission to do things, the freedom of being able to walk around in your underwear without any complaints.

Paul knew he could have done a lot worse than Mr. Tangredi, and because of that, he is grateful for his generosity. The fact that the house Paul lived in was not his own did bother him. Paul had saved his money for the last couple of years and had his mind set on being a homeowner. It was always a dream of his to own his own home. After searching for a while, he finally found one that fits his budget, but his dreams turned into nightmares when the deal fell through, and the owners decided not to sell, plus the owners hit him with the bad news at the worst time. The closing date set, and Paul gave his landlord at the apartment he was renting notice he was leaving. Soon after, the landlord found a new tenant who had already given their security deposit and set to move in on the day after Paul proclaimed, he was leaving. Paul had all his things packed, but when it was time to sign the papers and transfer the deed, the owners had a change of heart at the last minute, and Paul was stuck with no place to live. So instead of renting a moving truck to move his things to his new home, on the day he planned to leave, he had to move his stuff to storage and stay in a motel that night.

Paul was devastated and aggravated. He met Mr. Tangredi at church and has known him for as long as he's been a member there, and that has been five years. One Sunday, Mr. Tangredi saw how disappointed and upset Paul looked, which wasn't normal for Paul because nine times out of ten, he is usually smiling. Concerned, he asked what was wrong then presented him with the idea of living with him until Paul found another home. Paul was angry about losing the house and felt like he was a burden for Mr. Tangredi, but he insisted Paul wouldn't be a problem. Paul stayed upset about losing his new home. Until he got laid off from his job, it was then when he realized it was good, he didn't get it to only lose it later. Paul realizes a bright side to it all was he still has his savings and receives $800 a month in unemployment compensation. Which is more than enough for where he's living, Mr. Tangredi only charges him $200 a month in rent and utilities. He didn't need the money. Mr. Tangredi just enjoyed the company. After his wife died, he didn't like living in his big house alone.

Paul not only had a furnished room but a private bathroom as well. Mr. Tangredi respected Paul's privacy and was a great roommate and an even better friend. All Mr. Tangredi mostly wanted from Paul was someone to hang out with. He treated Paul like the son he never had, which included some unasked Fatherly advice, but Paul didn't mind. He thought the whole situation turned out to be beneficial for him. At least Paul doesn't have to stress or rush in trying to find a new job. He has time to search for better and more permanent employment. Paul even considered going back to school and pursuing a degree in Business. Even though Paul isn't where he wants to be; still, he's thankful for where he is at in life because he knows it could always be worst.

Paul entered the kitchen and took off his button-down shirt and draped it over one of the chairs at the breakfast table, then walks over to the refrigerator. He grabbed his two-liter bottle of Tahitian Treat and poured a glass full. He retrieved the rest of his leftover chicken bog, it is a tasty southern meal made of boiled hen, rice, and cut up pieces of pork sausage. He made it for last night dinner and placed it in the microwave. As his food was warming, he took his drink with him into the living room and collapsed down on the couch, he sighed and thought for a moment. He never forgot the scream he heard and the church's doors slamming this morning. He never did find the source of the sound. He left the church soon after saying goodbye to Pastor Henry, but when he returned that evening for the bible class, as he walked up the steps of the church, he could hear that same scream. He shivered as the sound replayed in his mind. ***There's no way I imagined that*** he thought. He had an uneasy feeling, he heard the ding from the microwave, letting him know his food was ready, but he suddenly lost his appetite. He knew what he heard earlier had to be another sign he had something important to do but was afraid to find out what it was. Whenever Paul feels afraid or upset to try to stop the feeling, he prays. He got on his knees in front of the sofa and started to pray.

"Dear Father, I'm..."

he was at a loss for words. Paul really could not explain what he was feeling and didn't know what to pray for; he stops and silently meditated. Fifteen minutes had passed while he meditated. Paul lifted his head and began to pray again,

"Dear Father, I am still not sure what it is you want me to do, but for whatever it is, all I ask is for the strength to endure it. In Jesus' name, I pray, Amen."

Paul got up from in front of the couch and went back into the kitchen. He decided to reheat his food and eat it anyway. When the microwave dinged again, Paul took his food and went back into the living room. He grabbed the remote and turned-on Mr. Tangredi's 60in flat screen TV. Mr. Tangredi had DIRECTV, so Paul flipped over to STARZ to find a movie to watch. It was 9:00 pm, and The Avengers was on. An hour into the movie, Paul found himself dozing off till finally, he fell asleep on the couch. He drifts off into a dream.

Paul opens his eyes and realizes he is lying face down in the free faller position on something soft but doesn't know what or where he is. He tries to get up but can't. Paul felt a weight lying on top of him. Not an overwhelming pressure, but as if someone is lying on top of him and covering him, only he can't see who it is. Paul can feel whoever's arms wrapped around his shoulders, but it felt more like they were hugging him than holding him down. Still, he has no idea who it could be. So, he lays there maneuvering his head looking around, trying to see where he is. Suddenly, a large bear-like creature emerges from the shadows. Unknowingly to him, it was the beast. Paul gasped. He has never seen such a thing and didn't know what to think of it. It looks at Paul and begins to pace back in forth in the corner it is standing in. Paul stares at it, trying to figure out what kind of animal it is, but it becomes clear that that thing, that being was not any animal he has ever seen. It moves a bit closer towards him, then stops walking and continues to pace in place. Paul feels the strong urge to run but still is unable to get up. The beast angrily stares with its glowing red eyes but does nothing but continues to pace back and forth. Whoever is lying on Paul, gently places their hand on his head in a way to tell him to lay back down. Paul did so and found himself getting sleepy, the fear he had of the beast begins to fade, and he felt a calmness. As he begins to fall asleep, he hears repeated twice, Mark nine and twenty-nine, Mark nine and twenty-nine.

As soon as he fell asleep in the dream, he woke up in real life. Paul found himself stretch out on the couch in the same free faller position he was in, in his dream. He rubbed his eyes and exhaled. Paul looked up at the TV and noticed the movie had gone off. He checked the time on the cable box and saw it was midnight.

"Mark nine and twenty-nine,"

he said to himself, Paul got up and grabbed his King James Bible off the coffee table where he laid it when he got home. He flipped over to that verse and read it aloud,

"And he said unto them; This kind can come forth by nothing but by prayer and fasting,"

He thought for a second, as he remembered that verse and the other verses leading up to that one. Mark nine and seventeen began the story of what led to Jesus, saying Mark nine and twenty-nine. One of the multitudes brought his son to Jesus, saying a "dumb spirit possessed him," and none of the disciples could cast the spirit out. So, Jesus cast out the "dumb spirit," and after he cast it out. The disciples asked why they weren't able to do it, and praying, and fasting was Jesus' answer. Paul thought about how he prays everyday anyway, but fasting was not something he frequently does, and when he had fast before, it was only a couple of days. Going forty days was the first time he's done that.

"This kind can come forth by nothing, but by prayer and fasting." He repeated.

Then it hit him. He knew what God wanted him to do.

"Somewhere, someone is suffering from an evil spirit, and he wants me to cast it out!"

He announced as if he had the correct answer to a trivia question. Paul's mind immediately went back to the beast in his dream. ***A devil? Is that what that thing was?***

Chapter Fourteen

Agali was restless, and his mind pained with anxiety. He tossed and turned on his sofa, till finally he laid flat on his back. He let out a frustrated sigh as he stared up at the ceiling. He rested one hand on his upset stomach, and the other arm draped on his head. He felt miserable. Later that afternoon, Madam Jay and Agali continued discussing his current situation involving Christina. Madam Jay noticed when Agali wasn't rambling and gave clear details to exactly what happened, she was able to get a better understanding of what was going on. She realized that maybe the spell was going as plan after all. Since Agali's main reason for casting the spell was to kill Torres, Madam Jay thought the spirits inside Christina would then use Christina to commit the murder. Nanja did say when that spell is used, someone always perishes. Madam Jay is convinced that it was the spirits plan all along. By her logic, it was no coincidence that Christina stepped on the dirt instead of Torres. Madam Jay felt once the spirits have carried out what they were conjured to do, she would be able to help Christina. She suggested to Agali that it would be best for him to avoid talking to anyone else who may visit the Sosa residence, the last thing he needed to do was to look suspicious. She also advised him to ignore the Sosa's home all together for the rest of the day and night. No more spying or peeking through open curtains with his binoculars, just wait until a few hours before early morning or "crackuhday" [before day] as she put it, around 2:00 am to go over to the Sosa's home. Agali hated that he couldn't at least peek and see what was going on over there. He thought that if he knew what was going on, maybe he could get a head start on the plan before it was 2:00 am.

The plan was to hide Torres' dead body, so when the police come to investigate, there would not be any hard evidence against Christina. Agali even wanted Madam Jay to spend the night at his house while they waited to carry out the plan. They brainstormed on what should be done to Torres's corpse once they got it. Madam Jay proposed burning the body, but Agali objected to the idea saying, the smoke and smell would raise his neighbor's suspicions. He thought it would be best to freeze him, chop him up and throw his remains in the Charleston Harbor. He has a deep freezer that he believed was big enough to hold whole chunks of body parts, especially after he removed the shelves. He had an ax; he went and sharpened it earlier that evening. It seems like a good enough plan, but one thing burdens him deeply, and that was time. He must do everything quickly before any of Torres' or Christina's friends come over. It was mostly Torres' friend, Josh, Agali was most worried about since he was the one who frequents there often. Agali would have to get the body out without anyone noticing quickly, and if the murder was extremely messy, there was that to clean up. Agali was going to do everything he could think of to protect Christina from being a suspect for her missing husband. He even thought to leave some of Torres' blood on their front door "welcome" mat and let drops of blood descend backward going down their porch and the steps. Making it as if after Torres was murdered, the killer then drugged him away. To do that would take strength, and surely the police could not believe Christina could overpower Torres and drag his body away. He is bigger than her short, small frame, and he is military trained. ***No, they won't believe it, that alone should find her to be innocent***, Agali was beginning to believe his plan was perfect, but time. Time was the problem; could he be able to do all of that in such a short amount of time? Before the sun came up, before his neighbors were up and out starting their days. Tomorrow morning is Thursday, a workday for most of the neighborhood. Agali wondered was it possible to clean a crime scene spotless without leaving any evidence connecting Christina to the murder, and sneaking Torres's dead body out the house all before anyone in the neighborhood starts their day. He had to…he is determined to at least try because Madam Jay also gave him another promise, that made going through all that trouble worth it. She told him that once she cleansed Christina from the evil spirits, she also had a love spell that would make Christina fall madly in love with Agali. Which is something Madam Jay thought Nanja should have known about instead of conjuring a spirit of jealousy? Madam Jay was puzzled by that at first until it hit her that Agali did want the husband dead, which could explain why Nanja chose such a drastic spell. When Madam Jay promised Agali, she could reverse Nanja's mistake, and he could finally get what he was longing for, Christina as his wife. With the love spell, he could get Christina to move out of the country. Leave everything and all her family behind so that it would just be him and her forever. The thought of finally having her, being able to have his way with her, for a second gave him much joy. Soon his joy turned into misery when that problem arose in his mind again…time.

Chapter Fifteen

Torres comes home from his long and repetitive day. He groans from his sore muscles as he limps through the front door. After getting off the phone with Christina that morning, Torres spent a lot of time on his phone, surfing the web, watching new videos uploaded on YouTube, downloading music that Josh insisted he needed to hear. All that activity he was doing on his phone, ran his battery completely down. It wasn't fully charged, after coming home last night from that uncomfortable dinner with Agali. Torres tossed his phone on the coffee table and continued playing the Call of Duty game he had saved on his Xbox One wireless adapter. It was that morning when he realized he had forgotten his phone in the living room. Torres only had about seventy percent of battery at the start of the day, and it wasn't until his break at work when he realized he forgot his charger. Josh only had his fancy wireless charger that, unfortunately, wasn't compatible with Torres' phone. It was completely dead by the time Amy started contacting him about Christina. Torres is Christina's emergency contact at work, so Amy called him repeatedly trying to reach him, trying to find out what was wrong with Christina and was she alright. Since Torres's battery was dead, his phone was off, and Amy's calls went straight to voicemail. Amy left two voicemail messages, but it was useless cause Torres had no desire to check his phone that night, he was ready to relax. He had to get up early and start his day all over again. Torres knows emergencies arises, but in all his life, he would never have imagined what Christina experienced to happen. He saw the Escalade was not there and assumed Christina had not gotten home yet. It didn't worry nor upset him; it was only 6:36 pm. He figured Christina was out with some of the women from the therapy session she attended earlier. ***She's always for making new friends***, he thought. Torres smiled at the thought of Christina out having fun since she's been so stressed out these past few weeks. He went up to their bedroom and saw his phone charger lying on the bed. Torres was sure he put it in his duffle bag this morning, but apparently not. He grabbed it and connected it to the outlet behind the nightstand on his side of the bed. Torres hooked the phone to the charger and held down the power button to turn it on. He put the phone down on the nightstand as soon as he saw the light, and the T-Mobile logo appeared. Torres didn't even think to check to see if he had any missed calls. His mind couldn't focus on anything but getting ready for bed. He sat on the edge of the bed, untied and kicked off his heavy boots one by one, then started undressing. He couldn't wait to take a shower and wash off the dirt and sweat from his hard day. Torres got up and went out into the hall to the linen closet to get a towel when he hears the stairs creaking as if someone was walking on them.

"Hey, how was your day?"

He asked without looking away from the closet, thinking it was Christina. The creaking sound from the stairs stopped. He looked up, and no one was there, he walked over to the stairs and saw no one was on them.

"Christina! Baby, you home!"

There was no answer. Torres went back into the bedroom to find Christina, but no one was there.

"Christina?!"

He called again, still no answer. He left out the bedroom and walked down the stairs to try to find her. As he went towards the kitchen, the lights were off, and the only small light-emitting in the kitchen was from the digital clock display on the microwave, in that small light was a dark figure standing there breathing heavy, a deep inhale with a raspy exhale, almost like a low snarl. Torres stared at it for a moment, trying to see if the black silhouette were Christina, he took a closer look and realized it couldn't be her. It was a huge shape, and Christina was only a size four. He then thought maybe it was an intruder, so he swiftly moves in and quickly flipped on the lights. As soon as the light filled the room, the silhouette disappeared, and the sound of the heavy breathing stopped as well. Torres was stunned to find the kitchen empty. He looked all around it. The kitchen was not big, as soon as you walk in, on the left is the pantry door, a wraparound of countertops, and the stove, to the right was the refrigerator and the back door. In the center of the kitchen was the center aisle. The black figure Torres saw was standing in the middle behind the center aisle, and there's no way it could have gotten passed him without him noticing. The kitchen only had two entrances, and he was standing in one. The other was the back door, and Torres knew he would have seen and heard someone get out that way. He heard no footsteps or any movement when he rushed into the kitchen, but his own. It only took him three seconds to run in and flip on the lights. No way someone could have gotten out of his sight that fast. He paused a moment before deciding to go to the pantry to look inside even though he knew he would have seen or at least heard the opening and closing of the door if someone had entered it. Torres opened the pantry door, and of course, no one was inside. He left out the kitchen and began to search the rest of the house. Torres went into the living room, the den, and even the dining room. He came back to the kitchen to look again. He also checked both the back and front doors. Both doors were still locked.

"No one could have gone upstairs because I know I would have heard that," he told himself.

He stopped and listened to see if he could hear anymore movement in the house then realized no one else was there. Torres felt uneasy. He was sure he heard someone walking up the stairs and the heavy breathing in the kitchen.

"Damn, I'm tired. I need some sleep,"

he said, trying to convince himself it was just the imagination of a tired mind. Torres shook his head. He felt dumb for running around the house, looking for an intruder. He decided to brush off everything that happened and went to take his shower.

Torres dries off with the large blue one hundred percent cotton towel he had retrieved earlier from the linen closet and wrapped it around his hips just below his tight six-pack abs. Torres goes over to the dresser and pulls out a pair of boxers. He didn't bother putting on a pair of pajama bottoms. He saw some neatly folded beside his underwear. ***Why does Christina buy these for me? I barely wear them***. He thought. He closes the dresser drawer, turns, and walks over to the bed. He yanked back the comforter and flopped down face first. He turned his head and took in a deep breath and exhales an exaggerated but relaxing sigh, all he has on his mind is his hopes of going into a deep and restful sleep. He didn't even notice the blue light flashing on his phone, letting him know he has five missed calls.

Later that evening, at midnight, Torres was awakened from his restful slumber by an overwhelming heat. He pulled off the comforter. He was drenched in sweat, and the wet sheets were clinging to his skin. He kicked the rest of the covers off him and sat upright in the bed. He looked to Christina's side of the bed and saw a large lump underneath the comforter.

"Christina, I know you don't have the heat on?"

Torres mumbled while wiping the sweat off his face, still drowsy. No one answered him.

"Christina, Christina, you can't possibly be cold?"

Still, no response, the lump underneath the comforter, was completely still and silent.

"Babe, wake up."

Torres reached out and touched the lump to shake Christina awake, but as soon as he touched it, it jerked violently for a few moments then went back to being completely still.

"Christina?"

He snatched back the comforter. He jumped at what he saw. It was Christina, but she was bent completely backward. Christina's torso was towards Torres. Her head in the opposite direction. The heels of her feet rest on her breast. The soles and toes were on the top of her stomach. The back of her head lay on her buttocks. Her arms were pulled straight back underneath and between her body and legs. She was sound asleep in that position. Torres quickly got up to turn on the light to make sure he was seeing what he thought he was seeing. As soon as the lights come on, Christina's eyes popped open. Torres's heart dropped when he saw her eyes. Christina's eyes were no longer "pink eye" looking red. They were completely blood red and glowing; you could no longer see her iris.

"Christina?" Torres quivered at the sight of her.

"Turn off the light," She uttered.

"Christina, what…what the hell, why are you bent like that, what are you doing?"

Torres was dazed, his heart beats rapidly; he has known Christina ever since he was a teenager, and he has never seen her like this. He didn't know what to think, say, or do. Christina utterly ignored Torres's questions and repeated her request,

"I said, turn off the light," she spoke louder and clearer.

"No, Christina get up now and stop ok, I'm serious if you are playing a joke, you win."

Torres didn't know if what he saw was real, was it a dream or was Christina playing a practical joke whatever it was he wanted it to be over. Christina starts to growl. Then an inhuman voice emerges from her and yells,

"TURN OFF THE DAMN LIGHT!"

The light bulbs burst, and the room-darkens, Torres jumped, his back pressed against the bedroom door, he wanted to run but the fact that it was his wife, terror and sadness had complete control of his legs, paralyzed with fear. The only light that was in the room was the streetlight from outside radiating through the open curtains. Christina slides out of bed and drops to the floor, she unfolded herself and lay straight as a board with her arms pinned straight down her sides, and she laid face down on the floor. Torres trembles, his heart raced so he could hear the pounding of it in his ears. He takes short quick breaths like he's about to hyperventilate as he watched Christina waiting to see what she'll do next. She suddenly lifts her head.

Her eyes changed from glowing red to the black eyes of a serpent. She looks over at Torres then started slithering snakelike across the floor and enters the master bathroom. The door slams closed behind her. The inhuman sound that came out of her before bellowed in the bathroom with a loud shriek. Torres cringed from the horrible sound, his eyes began to tear up, and he was on the verge of being hysterical. ***Oh my God, oh my God, what the fuck is going on! She's sick, she's just sick, that's it, but can sickness change the sound of your voice?*** Torres' face went pale as a ghost at that thought. ***Sickness can't make your eyes change colors and glow. Can it?***

"What's wrong with my wife?" he whispered.

Torres took some deep breaths to calm down, he finally got the courage to move from his frozen fear-stricken state. He thought it was best to run. He convinced himself that this was not his wife he just saw and knew he needed help. Torres swiftly grabs his pair of pants that luckily for him, he left out on the floor and snatches his keys off the dresser, then darted out the bedroom. Torres got downstairs as fast as he could; as he rushed to get his pants on, he stumbled around and had one leg in and the other one out. Torres tripped and fell to the floor. He finished getting his pants on while sitting on the floor. He was trying to hurry just in case Christina came downstairs. The thought of being terrified of his wife made his apprehension worst.

"Ok, ok, I just need some help,"

He tries to put his emotions at ease. Torres gets on his feet and runs to the front door,

"I'll just drive over to Josh's and have him come back with me."

He opens the door and closes it behind, he ran down the porch steps, then stood still,

"Where's the car…"

Chapter Sixteen

Agali's weariness outweighed his worry as he fights to keep his eyes open; he loses the battle when he begins to doze off. About twenty minutes had passed, and Agali had fallen into a deep sleep. He's startled awake from a loud crash in the kitchen. He dismissed it at first, thinking it was just Madam Jay getting a glass of water or possibly finding something to eat, and in the process, she accidentally dropped something. He turned over on his side and was about to go back to sleep when low growls emerge from behind him. Agali quickly turns and looks behind. He remembered the sound. He heard it before when he was doing the ritual. He sat upright on the couch, tossed his feet to the floor, and listened. The growls continued in the kitchen and grew louder. The noises would remind you of the warning snarls a wolf makes when it's guarding its territory. Agali hesitated a moment before he finally stood up and slowly made his way to the kitchen. He gently pushed the kitchen swing door open slightly so that he could peek behind it. He was checking to see if those growls were coming from somewhere near the door.

When he saw the coast was clear, he entered through the swing door, as Agali walked in he saw there at the table was Christina, sitting with her back towards the door, and her head hung low. Her long hair was no longer neatly pressed and shiny, but matted and dirty. Instead of the white midi dress, she wore to the therapy session. She had on a white knee-length cotton nightgown that looked more brown than white as if she had been playing in the mud all day. Agali stood there, puzzled at the sight of her. So many questions filled his mind. ***How did she get so dirty? Are the growls coming from her? And more importantly…how did she get in here?*** He looked towards the back door in the kitchen. He thought the crash he heard earlier was when Christina broke in. He saw the door was still closed, and among further investigating, he saw it was still locked with the deadbolt lock latched.

Agali directed his attention back towards Christina. His heart pounded; he didn't know what to expect. Agali was afraid to go near her, fearing she would hit him again…or worst. Christina sat completely still, with her body slumped in the chair.

"Christina?" He called out but she didn't answer.

Christina didn't flinch. It was like she was dead, and someone positioned her in that chair. Even though Agali was afraid she would hurt him, he was more worried about her than himself. He walked towards her, thinking he should probably get Madam Jay. ***But what if she's gone by the time I come back. I'll grab her then convince her to go upstairs with me***, he thought. Agali stood directly behind her. He slowly reached his hand out to touch her shoulder. The moment his hand touched her, she sat up. It was like a scene in a science fiction movie. When the mad scientist flips the switch on the back of the robot, he created, and it comes alive. When Agali rested his hand on Christina's shoulder, it was as if her switch got flipped. Agali quickly snatched his hand back. Christina began to twist her torso all the way around without moving her legs, Agali winced at the sound of her spine snapping and her joints dislocating as just the top part of her body turns around. She stared up at him with those glowing red eyes. Agali turns and bolts out of the kitchen. He made it as far as the middle of the living room when Christina appears before him—levitating five feet off the floor. Agali trembled. He backs away from her, trying to go back to the kitchen and escape out the back door. He pushed the swing door but couldn't get it to open. He proceeded to slam his body against the door, but it didn't move. He stopped and pressed his back against the door, frozen in fear. His breathing quickens. He looked around, trying to find a different way to escape, but there wasn't anywhere to go without passing Christina, and he didn't want to go near her. Christina's body just hung in the air motionless. Agali looked passed her, looking at the front door. It was ten feet away from her, he thought for a second, it was either stand there and hope that she leaves on her own by which he doubted that would happen or try to pass her and get the hell out of that house. Agali decided to go for it. He took a step forward, but as soon as he moved, Christina lifts her head again, showing those glowing red eyes. Agali froze. He knew then he had made a mistake. He tried one last time to push open the swing door. When suddenly, Christina opens her mouth, and the joints in her jaw began to dislocate as the large fangs grew in on the top and bottom rows of her teeth. She lunged forward, flying across the room towards Agali.

"CHRISTINA DON'T!" He screams. Christina let out an ear-piercing screech.

Agali jumps up from the couch and falls on the floor; he looked around wildly and saw he was alone in the living room. Christina was nowhere in sight. He gasped for breath, drenched in sweat, the banging on his front door woke him from his horrifying nightmare. Agali manages to get on his feet, still dazed from his terrible dream. He first runs to the kitchen, making sure it was just a nightmare, and Christina was not there. He pushed open the swing door and stood in the doorway and saw the kitchen was empty. No one was around but him. The banging on his front door continued. He goes to open the front door before even stopping to check the peephole to see who it was. Agali was still stunned from his nightmare that seemed so real. He flung open the door, and his jaw dropped when he saw it was Torres.

Agali was speechless. He looked at Torres like he just saw a ghost. He could not believe he was still alive. Madam Jay and him both thought the spirits were going to kill him. This changes everything; all their plans to get rid of Torres' dead body were ruined. Agali was about to catch a serious attitude with him until he notices how visibly shaken Torres was. He stood at Agali's front door, trembling.

"What's wrong?" Agali asked.

Torres was hesitant to answer. He did not want Agali to know what exactly was going on. Besides, Torres didn't know if he could explain what was wrong anyway. All he knew was Christina scared the crap out of him. Torres kept looking back over at his home, worried Christina was going to come out of there any minute, crazed with a knife in her hand trying to attack him. He didn't want to be out there by himself, and he also didn't want to be around Agali. Torres didn't know or talk to any of his other neighbors well enough to make an uninvited visit to their homes this time of the night. Torres pondered over the thought of going over to Agali's house for about ten minutes before he came, the more he stood outside alone; however, the more afraid he became. Torres soon realized he was desperate, and he figured Agali's company is better than being outside alone.

"Can I come in, please?" Torres's voice was shaky.

He knew he needed to calm down a little, so he won't have to go into detail of what was happening at his house to Agali. Agali stepped aside and allowed Torres to enter in. Madam Jay, dressed in her bathrobe, descended the stairs. The pounding on the front door woke her. "`Smattuh?" [What is the matter] She asked.

"Yes, Torres, what brings you by this time of night, and where's Christina?" Agali probed.

"Um," Torres's mind blanked. To hear Christina's name scared him all over again.

"We had a fight." He finally answered.

"A fight?" Agali questioned.

"Yes, you know married couples have their disagreements from time to time, and tonight we had one."

Torres tries to think quickly on his feet. Agali and Madam Jay just looked at each other while Torres continued.

"Yeah, and I am sorry to disturb you with this at this time of the night. I just came over to ask you, do you know a faster way to get to JBC without taking the interstate?"

Torres pulled that question out his ass. He knew how to get there and felt the interstate was the fastest way since that's the way Josh always took but couldn't think of anything else to ask Agali.

"No, I do not, is there any reason why you could not have search for that answer on your GPS instead of coming to my home at 1:30 am?"

"Um, I tried, and I'm having problems with my internet I needed to know so I can tell the cab driver what direction to take."

"A cab? Don't you have a vehicle?" Agali asked.

"Yes, I do," ***At least I hope I still do***. Torres thought, wondering what happened to his SUV. "But Christina took it to a friend's house…that's where she's at, and I'm going over there. I was going to wait until morning, but I can't wait any longer."

"Why don't you take my car." Agali offered.

Even though borrowing Agali's car sounds like a good idea. Torres still refused.

"No, thank you, man, hey, you know I don't have my phone on me, instead of walking all the way home to get it, do you mind if I use yours real quick to call that cab?"

Torres continues to mention the cab hoping Agali would insist on letting him borrow his car. Torres felt terrible for needing to borrow Agali's car. That was a big favor to ask someone you're not related to or even friends with. Especially someone he had no intention of ever talking to again must less going over to their home and borrowing their things. Torres believes Agali is a weird person, to say the least, and Agali gave him this uneasiness like maybe he shouldn't have come to his home, but again Torres was desperate. Torres felt stuck between a rock and a hard place. It was either deal with the uneasiness and negative energy that came off Agali or go back to his home alone with a wife that has something seriously wrong with her.

"Yeah, I will just call a cab, and I'll be out of your hair." Torres cleared his throat and gave a nervous smile.

"No, I insist, trust me this town isn't like the big city where taxi cabs are plentiful, getting a cab at this time of the night will be close to impossible, just let me grab my keys. Please have a seat."

Torres had a slight feeling of relief that Agali granted such a huge favor. He left his wallet at home and had no intention of going back in there by himself, and if he had gotten the cab, he intended to ask Josh to pay it for him. Which is something Josh would not have been happy about. It was either bum off Josh or walked twelve and a half miles to his house. Either way, Torres was not going back home now. Besides, he also needed a few moments to sit and think about what he is going to do next even after he gets Josh. Agali left the room, and Madam Jay followed behind.

"Wuh are oonuh up tuh, oonuh cyan' b'leew dat story bout dem habing uh fight?" [What are you up to, you cannot believe that story about them fighting] She asked.

"I know he is lying, but since he is still alive, we have to get rid of him somehow so we can go get her."

"Are oonuh gwine tuh kill'um?" [Are you going to kill him] Madam Jay probed.

"No, that won't be necessary now, when he leaves, we go over and get Christina, and by the time he comes back we will be done, and I'll be ready to take her away from here."

"É don' wu'k dat fast, wuh ef é come' yuh and see um gone?" [It doesn't work that fast, what if he come here and see her gone]

"Don't worry, I know we will have plenty of time now."

"Enty?" [Is that so]

"Follow me. I'll show you."

Agali leads Madam Jay through the kitchen to go out of the back door. Agali made sure to open and close the door quietly so Torres wouldn't know they had gone outside. They walked around his house to the front yard to his car, a 2009 Honda Pilot.

"Oh, just a moment, I forgot something?"

Agali ran back behind his house to his shed and came back to the front yard where Madam Jay stood waiting beside his car. He went over to the rear driver side tire.

"Wuh iz è oonuh were gwine tuh show me?" [What is it you were going to show me] Madam Jay asked.

"Look at him. He doesn't have anything on him. He's not wearing a shirt and no shoes. It looks like he just grabbed his pants and ran out of there. Whatever happened over there scared him bad, and as shaken as he looks, I doubt he goes back over there right now."

"So," Madam Jay responded, wanting Agali to get to the point.

"So, this is my plan."

Agali had a nail and hammer in his hand. He took the nail and drove it into his back tire.

"While he's out on the highway, he'll have a flat tire. You heard him say he doesn't have his phone on him and I don't know for sure but I doubt he took his wallet with him, plus it's almost 2:00 am everything is closed so he will be out for a while dealing with that flat tire. Giving us plenty of time to do what we have to do."

"Aww clever, leggo quickly b'fo' de tire go flat yuh." [Aww clever, let's go quickly before the tire deflates here]

"Just one more thing I need to remove the spare tire, this may take a minute could you go in and distract him please Madam."

Madam Jay nodded her head "yes" and quickly headed back around the house, while Agali begins opening the hex nut to lower the spare tire from under the car. Madam Jay enters through the back door. Again, creeping in continuing to make sure that Torres is unaware they were plotting something. Madam Jay casually walks into the living room, she catches Torres' glance and nods her head forward at him as her way of saying "hello."

"É dunkyuh 'bout oonuh, é leabe oonuh." [She doesn't care

about you; she leaves you]

Madam Jay remarked, trying to strike a conversation with him.

"Huh,"

Torres wanted her to repeat what she said. He didn't know whether it was he didn't hear her, or he didn't understand her.

"É dunkyuh 'bout oonuh, é leabe oonuh." Madam Jay repeated. [She doesn't care about you, she leaves you.]

Torres just nodded his head to acknowledge her, he still didn't understand anything she just said, but he didn't have the patience or energy at that moment to try to figure it out. Agali rushed into the living room and handed Torres the keys. Torres thanked Agali, said "see you later" to Agali, and Madam Jay then hurried off, he wanted to go get Josh and make it back as fast as he could so he can check on Christina. Madam Jay and Agali went out and stood on the steps to watch Torres leave. As he sped away, Madam Jay looked at Agali and stated,

"Oonuh know dribing luh dat on uh bad tire could kause uh serious accident." [You know driving like that on a bad tire could cause a serious accident]

"That would be fine too," Agali responded. They both looked at each other with devilish grins.

Chapter Seventeen

Agali and Madam Jay go inside then go their separate ways. Agali looks down at his watch to time how long he thinks Torres will take. It is now 1:57 am, Agali goes to his back yard to his shed to gather some things he felt he would need to break into the Sosa's home. Madam Jay headed upstairs to get dressed. As time drew near for them to go and "cleanse" Christina from the evil spirits that have Christina captive, Madam Jay begins to have second thoughts. She thinks back to earlier yesterday when she saw Christina for the first time. It was a sight Madam Jay felt she would never forget. In all her years of being a root worker, never has she ever experienced a case like this. At first, Madam Jay was eager to help Agali. The money he offered drew her interest, but now she wonders have she gotten herself into something she's not ready to handle. After Agali invited her to spend the night, she went home to grab a few things for the overnight stay, and the items she needed for the cleansing and love spell she agreed to put on Christina for Agali. She threw everything together in a burlap sack. She opened the sack to get her white shirt and black skirt. She quickly got dressed then decided to double-check to make sure she had everything. As she looked through her sack, she noticed a small leather bag. In her haste to grab everything, she accidentally threw in her bag of possum bones.

The bones she used for her bone readings. She used them as her way of seeking information from the spirits. They were for fortune-telling. Some root workers use tarot cards for their divination. Others use both bone readings and tarot cards, but Madam Jay is old-school and liked the bone readings way better. The common bones used are chicken and possum bones. Madam Jay and her people use possum bones. When she saw the bones, her heart sank to her stomach. She regretted she didn't look in her sack sooner and discovered the bones were in there. Madam Jay believes it is important to first ask the spirits permission before performing any spell. She could not believe she had forgotten something that important. To do her bone reading, she needs to be outside and draw a circle in the dirt. Nowadays, most root workers have a more modern way of doing bone readings and going outside wasn't necessary. Again, Madam Jay was old-school, and the outside way was the traditional way her people did it and how she learned it. Agali had a well-kept lawn, so for her to draw a dirt circle, she must first rip up a patch of grass. Madam Jay could put a piece of goatskin on the ground to throw the bones on it; unfortunately, she didn't have any with her. The real problem is bone reading isn't a quick process; in fact, it's a ritual itself. It would have been better for her to do it earlier while Agali was busy getting things ready for tonight. She had time alone, but now that he is waiting on her, her time was limited. Besides, even with the trap set for Torres, there's no guarantee he will be gone for a very long time. She also knew there was absolutely no way she could convince Agali to do this another day. He was determined to get Christina as soon as possible before it was too late. Madam Jay sighs and sits down on the edge of the bed. She can't fault him for his rush. Christina's situation was like none of her other clients she's helped before. She has done curse removals and jinx-breaking spells, but after seeing Christina, it was obvious that this was more than someone experiencing bad luck.

"É iz possessed," [She's possessed]

Madam Jay said aloud, staring blankly while in deep thought. Demonic possession is only something she knew of but never done a case involving it. Madam Jay takes a trip down memory lanes as she remembers her friend Charles, who died trying to free his beloved sister Susan from her possession. Charles died of a heart attack; the stress of it all was too much for him. Susan never did get the help she needed. A couple of weeks after Charles's heart attack, Susan slit her own throat, right after she brutally murdered her husband. Madam Jay swallowed hard, and goosebumps covered her arms as she remembered Susan. Her mind then flashes back to Christina's cold glares staring at her through Agali's kitchen window. Chills ran down her spine when she thought about those glowing red eyes. Madam Jay shakes her head, snapping out of her trance about Susan and Christina. The best thing she felt to do is to tread lightly on the whole situation. Madam Jay has a strong belief in what she does. After a moment of doubt, she changes her mind to a more positive outlook and realizes if she just does her spells as normal and conjures the right spirits to help her, everything will work out. Madam Jay reached back into her sack to grab and put on her protection necklace. Made of twine string and the breastbone of a pied kingfisher. It was a charm known to keep evil spirits away. She always wore it in every spell she performed as a form of protection. When casting spells of vengeance, there's always a risk in contacting dangerous and unwanted entities. Madam Jay figured if the charm protected her then it would protect her in this case. She knelt on the floor, grasping the bag of possum bones in one hand and with the other, made a tight fist around her charm. She closed her eyes, and begin to recite out loud the Lord's prayer,

"We Papa een heaben, leh ebrybody hona you nyame cause you da holy. We pray dat soon you gwine rule oba all ob we. Wasoneba ting you da want, leh dey een heaben, Gee we de food wa need dis day yah an ebry day. Fagibe dem people wa do bad to we. Leh we don't habe haad test wen Satan try we. Keep we from e ebil."

[Our Father which art in heaven, Hallowed be thy name. Thy Kingdom comes, Thy will be done, as in Heaven, So in earth. Give us day by day our daily bread. And forgive us our sins; for we also forgive every one that is indebted to us. And lead us from evil.] [Luke 11:2-4 KJV]

She quickly opened her eyes, startled by the rapid knocks on the bedroom door. Agali opens the door and walks halfway in.

"Madam, are you ready?"

Madam Jay let out a sigh of relief when she saw it was just Agali. She took a deep breath and exhaled it while standing up on her feet.

"Leggo." [Let's go] she answered.

It was now 2:30 am, Agali and Madam Jay stood on his front doorsteps. He had turned off all the lights, including the outside porch lights by the front and back doors. They stood in the dark for a moment, listening to see if anyone else was up or outside. The lights were out in every home surrounding the Sosa's residence, and the only sound heard was the chirping of the crickets. Which implied the other neighbors were either fast asleep or weren't home. They were as calm as they could be. Agali and Madam Jay try not to look obvious that they were up to something. They hurried and made their way to the Sosa's porch, then ducked behind the porch swing. Both looked around one more time, making sure no one saw them. Luckily for them, the lights were out at the Sosa home, including the porch light. Agali reached in his pocket for his keys, to get his mini-LED key light on his key chained. He clicked on his light and started searching through his black duffle bag, he earlier filled with tools to use to break in the Sosa's home. As he searched through his duffle bag, Madam Jay panned their surroundings. Agali stopped his search for a second and huffed in disappointment. He wished he had planned this break-in better. When Agali went through his tools, he realized everything he had would make too much noise while using it. This being a quiet neighborhood. Drilling on someone's door at this time of the night would draw nothing but suspicion and maybe even a call to the police. He again let out an exaggerated sigh and shook his head. Madam Jay saw the look of defeat on Agali's face. Agali had the expression of a basketball player missing the winning shot. She was about to ask him what was wrong until she notices Agali was inadvertently holding the flashlight outwards, and the light shined on the front door. It was open.

"Look uh der!" [look]

Madam Jay exclaimed in a loud whisper. Agali directed his attention to where she was pointing. A smile came across his face.

"Finally, something is going right tonight."

He whispered as he stands to his feet. Agali helps Madam Jay up, and they both slowly made their way to the front door as soon as Agali's hand gripped the doorknob. Madam Jay grabbed his forearm.

"Wait, oonuh git somet'ng tuh hol' é?" [Wait, you got something to hold her?] She asked.

"Shit, I completely forgot! Just when I thought the night was getting better."

Agali was starting to get aggravated with the whole situation but knew he needs to get it done.

"Well, maybe I could talk her into coming with us, and if not, then she's not that big, the two of us together should be able to take her."

Madam Jay thought Agali's idea was terrible. She remembered him telling her earlier that when Christina slapped him, it was like she had the strength of a "linebacker." There was no way she could take on Christina, possessed, or not. Madam Jay is an older woman and doesn't have the strength she used to have. Nevertheless, Madam Jay doesn't say anything but nodded her head in agreement.

Chapter Eighteen

Agali enters the home first, and Madam Jay follows in closely behind him. As soon as they made it through the front door, they were hit with a horrible smell. The scent of raw putrid meat lingered in the air.

"OH!" Madam Jay exclaimed, gagging from the odor.

She covered her nose and mouth with her hand. Agali gripped the neck of his t-shirt and pulled it over his nose, trying to stifle the scent in the room. The house was pitch-black, Agali closed the front door and flipped the light switch that was beside it. Nothing happened. He clicked on his mini flashlight, using the light of it to guide him on to one of the lamps sitting on top of one of the end tables in the living room. He clicked the switch under the lampshade, but again nothing happened. He and Madam Jay continued with only the light from the flashlight to see. They made their way into the kitchen where Madam Jay tries to turn on the lights, but flipping the light switch was pointless because the lights stayed out. Agali looked around the kitchen and noticed even the small light that would have emitted from the digital clock display on the microwave was out. Seeing the black space where clock would have been, reminded him he needed to keep up with the time. He shines the flashlight at his wrist to check his watch again. It is now 2:48 am. ***The power must be out.*** He thought. What made it even eerier was the streetlights that shine near the Sosa's home were out as well. There were two, one in the front of the house and the other for the street behind their house. The one in front of the home was across the street. If it were on, a little light would shine on the lawn and beam behind the mini blinds in the living room. The streetlight in the back of the home was the closes, and if it were on, some light would shine through open curtains. Since no lights were shining on or near the home, it made the inside of it even darker. If Agali didn't have his mini flashlight, he and Madam Jay wouldn't even be able to see their own hands in front of their faces. Agali has lived in that neighborhood for the past fifteen years and realizes he has never seen both streetlights out. ***You would usually see one out every few blocks, but to have two out at the same time and place. Also, why is their power out? My lights are on, and we share the same power line, maybe the cable that's connected to their home is broken.***

"It can happen, but very unlikely." He mutters to himself.

"Huh," Madam Jay heard the mumble and responded.

"Nothing," Agali shook his head. "Let's hurry and find her."

They left out of the kitchen with Agali still leading the way. They continued upstairs. The stairs creaked as they ascended them, so they paused every other step, trying not to make too much noise. They didn't want to alarm Christina that they were inside. They wanted to make a gentle and easy approach, so they wouldn't accidentally frighten her to anger. When they reached the top of the stairs, Agali looked both ways down the dark hallway. There were three doors to the left and two to the right. The doors to the right were the closes to the stairs, so he decided to go to the right first to start his search for Christina.

The last door at the end of the hallway, Agali opened first. It was one of the three bedrooms, filled with open and unopen boxes. Torres and Christina use this room as mini storage until they can agree on what to make of the empty room. The debate was between Torres wanting to turn it into his home gym while Christina wants a home office. Agali flashed the light around the room when he saw Christina was not there. He continues to the next door. The narrow door across from the third bedroom was the linen closet. Agali took a glance in it then went on down the hall to the next door. The second bedroom. This room was empty, Torres and Christina were saving this room for their future child. Agali again took another glance as it was obvious nothing or no one was in there. Madam Jay just walked quietly behind him while holding on to his arm. She was having a hard time seeing in the dark, and she was also incredibly nervous. Not being able to see in front of you or behind was nerve-wracking.

Agali reaches the fourth door. He swung it open to only reveal the second bathroom. It was spotless and still had the "new house" smell because Torres and Christina never use it. There was a full bathroom connected to the master bedroom. So, they decided to make the second one for guests only. Since no guests have visited yet, except for Josh, it still hasn't been used much. They have only been living in the home for a little over a month. Neither one of their families has visited yet. Agali saw the barely used bathroom, and it triggered a thought. ***It's a shame how this nice house will go to***

waste. Once I take Christina as mine, Torres will be here all alone. Oh well, he can remarry. Agali just shrugs as his way of saying he does not care about Torres. His selfish desires blind him from how evil he is towards Torres. Agali closes the door and looks ahead to the last room in the hallway.

"Here's the master bedroom,"

Agali says to Madam Jay pointing in the direction of the last door on the hall. As they walked closer to the bedroom, they started hearing movement inside.

"Christina!" Agali called out, but no answer.

They crept closer and closer to the master bedroom door. They could hear footsteps in the bedroom like someone was pacing the floor.

"Christina!"

Agali called out again. And again, no response. He knocks on the door. After his knocks, Agali and Madam Jay looked at each other when they notice the footsteps stop. Hesitant, he didn't know what to expect. Agali wondered was Christina going to be quick-tempered like she was the other morning, or worse, will she be the way Agali saw her in his nightmare. Agali swallows hard and listens closely to see if he could hear anything. Madam Jay stares at Agali, awaiting his next move. When the footsteps stopped, and Agali and Madam Jay stood still, the house was silent. The only sound in the entire house was the rapid heavy breathing of them both. They were overwhelmed with nervousness. After a moment of listening and getting the courage to continue, finally, Agali grips the doorknob and turns it.

Madam Jay makes a tight fist around her protection charm and takes a deep breath. He opens the door and shines the light inside; there, standing six feet away from the door, is the beast. It's down on all fours, crouching and snarling, showing its very large fangs, and its long black shiny hair is now wet with blood, and it drips off its body. It just crouches there, glaring with those piercing glowing red eyes. Without thinking, both Agali and Madam Jay turn and run. As Agali's arms pumped while he ran, the light from the flashlight bounced all around facing upward, so there wasn't any light in the direction of where they were going. They ran blindly down the dark hallway, trying to make it to the stairs, but before they even made it to the stairs.

Madam Jay trips and falls, and Agali stumbles and falls over her. They both fell face down to the floor. Panic and fear-stricken, Agali snatched the flashlight that fell out of his hand in the fall from off the floor and bolted to his feet to look back to see if the beast was behind them, but the beast was no longer in sight. He flashed the light towards the bedroom. In his quick escape, he left the door wide open. When he flashed the light inside the room, he saw the beast wasn't in the place it was before. He shined the light all around him, searching for it but didn't see it. However, he did find out what it was that Madam Jay tripped over. He reached down and helped Madam Jay to her feet. They both stared down; there sitting on the floor in front of them was Christina. She was what tripped Madam Jay. Christina sat on the floor, first whimpering then begins to weep harder, the tears flow down her face. She sat on the floor, hugging her legs, rocking back and forth. Agali was so happy to see her that he didn't even notice that Christina was not in the hallway before, it was like she just appeared. However, Madam Jay noticed, the first and only thing they have seen since they been in that house was the beast. Now it's gone and all of a sudden Christina appears.

The thought of that was starting to make Madam Jay even more uneasy. Agali shines the flashlight directly on Christina. She turns away from the brightness of it. He approaches her and squats down in front of her. Agali gently grips her chin and lifts her head to get a good look at her. He shines the light at her chest instead of her face so that the light wouldn't hurt eyes. Still gripping her chin, Agali moved Christina's face towards his, when she looks up at him, he saw her blood-red eyes. Her iris was no longer visible; both of her eyes were blood red entirely. It was like the blood vessels in both her eyes broke, and the blood washed over the entire eye. Agali gasped and quickly snatched his hand away from her face. He stands to his feet; flashes the light over towards Madam Jay, who still is holding onto her protection charm. He looks back at Christina and saw she still had on the midi dress she wore to the therapy session. Only when she first put it on yesterday morning, it looked brand new. It was only her second time wearing it, but now it's dingy, dirty, and tattered from her thighs down. The dress looked as if she has worn it for years and never took it off. Agali also notices how bad she smelled, but it wasn't a natural body odor, but the stench of rotting flesh.

"Christina, are you ok?"

Agali asked, wrinkling his nose from the awful smell as he moves closer to her. Christina took in a deep breath then let it out slowly. The tears were streaming down her face.

"Torres, Torres…" She mumbled.

"No, it's me, Agali."

"Wh-where's Torres?" She trembled.

"I don't know, I saw him leaving in a black pickup truck earlier," Agali lied. The black pickup truck he was referring to was Josh's truck.

"I need…you have to find him, I…"

"Now, now, calm down." he shushes her.

Agali could hear the pain in Christina's voice and felt that it was her talking. He moves away from Christina and softy tugged Madam Jay over towards him.

"I think it's still Christina. The spell hasn't taken her completely yet." He whispered in her ear. "It has changed her appearance, but not her mind."

"No, don' b'leew é." [No, don't believe it] Madam Jay warned.

In Madam Jay's mind, this was Susan all over again. There was still the mystery of how Susan got possessed in the first place. Madam Jay shook her head.

"De sperrits deceibing, look uh der é eyes…é gone." [The spirits are deceiving, look at her eyes…she's gone]

The longer Madam Jay was around Christina, the more nervous she became. She realized in all her years in practicing root work and all the clients she had. Madam Jay has never been this afraid before. This situation she has gotten herself into was way more than she has ever experienced.

"No, it's not too late, we're doing this!" Agali snapped.

He huffed; Madam Jay's words were starting to give him a headache. He refused to believe her. After all, he has done to get Christina. There was no way he was going to give up now. Madam Jay shook her head no,

"Leggo," [let's go] she urged.

She was tugging on his arm to leave. Agali angrily snatches himself away from her and goes back over to Christina.

"I'm going to help you. This lady here,"

he points at Madam Jay then shines the light on her so Christina could see her.

"This lady is a doctor, and she's going to help you and make you better."

Christina looked dazed, Agali wasn't even sure if she had understood what he just said. She stopped crying for a second and gazed up at him with those blood-red eyes. Agali broke her gaze. He was starting to get creeped out by the sight of her eyes. He was telling himself that it's just the spell, and after the spiritual cleansing, everything will be fine. ***She'll be back to normal soon,*** he thought.

"I need you to come with us…ok?"

He moved his hand to Christina's head and rubbed it in a comforting way. When he attempted to run his fingers through her hair, he saw how tangled it was. Christina's hair no longer had that silky, smooth, straight, and shiny look to it, but it was filthy and matted up. Agali's hand felt wet after touching Christina's hair, so he moved his hand away from it, and shined the flashlight on it to see what was on it. Blood. There was blood in her hair, just like there was blood dripping off the beast's fur. Agali used the flashlight to check Christina's head for any open wounds but found none. Madam Jay notices Agali searching through Christina's hair and asked

"Wuh wrong?" [What's wrong]

"Nothing,"

Agali looked back at Madam Jay shaking his head. He knew something was not right but refuse to accept the fact that he may have lost Christina. He snaps out of his moment of disappointment when Christina began to cry harder. Agali then squatted beside her and put his arm around her. Christina then pressed her head against his chest. Agali changed his squatting position to placing his knees on the floor and wrapped both his arms around her. Holding her closely, he smiled at the thought of finally being able to have her in his arms.

"Uh-huh," Madam Jay cleared her throat. "Us mus' go." [We

must go] she demanded.

Agali was lost in the embrace that for a moment, he became nose blind to Christina's horrible smell. Finally, he nodded his head in agreement with Madam Jay that it was time to leave. He stood to his feet, then bent down to lift Christina. Agali cradles her in his arms as he carried her. Madam Jay took the flashlight and grabbed his black duffle bag off the floor and led the way while he brings Christina. When they make it to the front door, Madam Jay clicks off the flashlight and opens the door a bit to peek outside, looking to see if anyone was around. All the while Christina whimpers continues, Agali bounced and shushed her like a small child as he held her in his arms. He was overjoyed by the fact that he was holding Christina, the love of his life, that her whimpers didn't bother him. Madam Jay, on the other hand, would occasionally look back over her shoulder at Christina. Christina's crying was starting to annoy her. Madam Jay watches Agali as he holds Christina closely and gently rocks her trying to comfort her. It was then when Madam Jay realized how obsessed Agali is of Christina. He was sick, just the sight of Christina at that moment was disturbing, her wild matted hair, her dirty and tattered dress, she smelled horrible and worse of all her blood-filled eyes. No person in their right mind would even go near her, must less cradle her in their arms, and the smile Agali had on his face, while he rested his head on Christina's, was starting to creep Madam Jay out even more. Agali caught Madam Jay's stares, and his smile turns into a frown. She quickly looked away and directed her attention back outside. When she felt it was ok to continue, she motioned Agali to come. They quickly maneuvered from the Sosa's yard to Agali's yard. Christina shivered and sobbed. It was like the closer she got to Agali's house, the more afraid she became. Besides the whimpers, Christina hadn't made a sound since she questioned the whereabouts of Torres. Now, she begins to moan and groan like her body is tormented with pain; she starts kicking, trying to free herself from Agali's arms. She yells and flares about, trying her hardest to get away from him. Agali fights hard to gain control over her.

"Hurry up and open the door!" Agali shouted.

Madam Jay panics, Christina was now causing a scene, and she felt someone might hear her. Madam Jay was already nervous, and now she was getting jumpy, and Agali yelling at her was only making matters worse. Madam Jay was having a hard time trying to steady her hand to get the key through the lock on the front door. Finally, she got the door open, as soon as Agali stepped through the front door, Christina stops abruptly and goes limp in Agali's arms. Agali continues into the living room, staring at Christina, confused by the whole situation. Madam Jay takes a step closer to them, looking at Christina. Agali noticed Madam Jay out the corner of his eye.

"Hurry, close the door." He instructed.

Madam Jay rushed over to the door and slammed it close. Agali gently laid Christina on the sofa.

"Christina?"

He felt the side of her neck for a pulse. He found one. The vein in her neck was jumping fast, which meant her heart was beating rapidly, yet she was completely still, it was like she fainted. Seeing she was still alive, Agali dismissed it as she wore herself out with all the fighting and yelling, she just did.

Little did they know, when they found Christina, they thought she seem distracted, not aware of her surroundings. They figured the spell caused her delusional state. What they don't know is "Christina" was no longer present. Even when she asked about Torres, it wasn't Christina talking. Christina had blacked out a while ago and is now screaming for help inside her head. Before Agali and Madam

Jay arrived and just a little while after Torres left, Christina came to herself. She woke up in the fetal position inside her bathtub in the master bathroom. When Christina had awakened, she was out of breath, soaking wet with sweat, and cold. Christina's body trembles from the cold as she climbed out of the tub, she slowly walked towards the bathroom door, rubbing her hands up and down her arms, shaking, when Christina passes by the mirror, she stopped in her tracks, shocked at how terrible she looked. Her hair was sweated out and shrunk into an uneven afro, the appearance of her hair would remind you of buckwheat from the little rascals, but the bad hair day Christina was having isn't what stopped her and caused her to stare at herself in the mirror. Christina noticed she didn't see clearly; it was like she had blinders on the side of her head. The whites in her eyes were covered with blood and were starting to spread to her iris. She quickly turned away, the sight of herself, disturbed her so much that it was making her sick. She rubbed her stomach and rested against the sink. Christina jumped and gasped when she heard a thudding coming from the bedroom.

"Torres?"

She waits for a response and continues to listen. Her heart began to race.

"Torres, is that you? Answer me, please."

Christina slowly made her way to the bathroom door. The thudding continued, and she could hear unintelligible whispers. She shivers both in fear, and from being cold. When she opens the door, she slowly widens it, peering,

"Torres?"

The beast quietly stood in the middle of the bedroom on its hind legs. It was scowling at her, waiting on her to see him. When Christina makes eye contact with the beast, she shrieks in fear and tries to close the bathroom door, but a force snatches the grip of the door from her, pushes the door and keeps it wide open. Christina continues to scream; the beast gets off its hind legs and crouches to the floor. It takes a few steps closer to her. Overwhelmed with terror, she searches around, trying to find a way out. She moves towards the frosted window above the bathtub. Out of desperation, she tries to escape by climbing out the two-story window. Before she could make it to the tub, the same force that pushed the door open grabs Christina's ankles, slams her body to the floor and drags her out the bathroom to the beast.

Chapter Nineteen

Torres raced down west interstate 26 headed towards JBC, unaware of the booby trap Agali has set for him. The tire slowly deflates as he speeds down the highway. His heart and mind were racing. If he was a volcano and stress was lava, he would be erupting right now. His thoughts went from thinking of a way to explain what just happened to him to Josh, from wondering what is wrong with Christina and is she ok. When he approaches a sign that alerts him, his exit is on the right in two miles. He begins to slow down to merge into the right lane. That's when the SUV starts shaking violently.

"Come on, man, not now," Torres grumbled.

The more he decreases the speed, the more the SUV shook. He had been driving with the windows down since it was another humid night. Even in the early morning hours, the temperature was still in the 70s. As he slowed down, he could hear a loud popping sound coming from out the left driver's side window. The loud popping and the SUV shaking causes him to slow down even more, not wanting to continue, afraid he may lose control of the vehicle. He decides to pull over onto the shoulder. He puts it in park and clicks on the flashers. As soon as he exits the car, he immediately saw the bad tire on the rear driver's side. He goes and squats down beside it to get a better look. It was still dark out, and the only light around was the streetlights on both sides of the highway. Torres felt on his pants pockets looking for his phone, wanting to use the flashlight on it, forgetting he left it at home on the nightstand charging. He sucks air through his teeth and stands to his feet.

"FUCK!"

He slams his hand on the side of the car in frustration then goes back to the driver's side to turn the SUV off. He snatched the keys from the ignition and goes to the trunk and begins looking for the jack and spare tire. When he opens the trunk, he notices a handle in the trunk lining that lifts open, exposing a storage compartment. On the right side of it is where the jack kit is supposed to be, but unknowingly to Torres, Agali had already removed it before he left. The missing jack wasn't the only thing Torres notices; he also saw on the floor of the trunk that the hex nut was open. He got face down on the ground to look under the SUV and saw the spare tire was missing as well. Even though it was dark, he still could see some with the help of the streetlights. To be sure he reached underneath the car feeling the area of where the spare tire would have been, and felt the spot was empty.

Torres comes from underneath the vehicle to a seated position on the ground, resting his back against the SUV. He rests his arms on his knees and shakes his head.

"Either I'm having some fucked up luck, or I got setup. Amazing how his car gets a flat tire on the same day, the jack and spare tire are gone."

Torres needed to voice his anger. His mind couldn't handle another thought. He's going through a lot of emotions from being upset to flat out exhausted. If something good doesn't happen for him soon, he feels he might snap. Torres rubs his eyes, inhales a deep breath, and exhales heavily. The sound of a car pulling off onto the shoulder in front of him caught his attention. Blue lights flashed, to Torres' relief, it's the police. The police car was an all-black 2015 Dodge Charger with the word "Sheriff" in big gold letters on the sides of it. The cop exited the car with his large bright flashlight shining directly on Torres. Torres put his hands up to block the bright light from his eyes.

"You alright?"

The officer asked with a strong southern accent. He was a Caucasian man in his mid-40s, about six foot one, sturdy, with dark brown hair, and he carried a serious expression as if smiling was something he rarely did.

"No, I got a flat tire," Torres responds as he slowly stands to his feet.

"A flat tire?" the officer repeated.

He walks over to the SUV, examining it. The officer sees the deflated tire and shines his light on it, that's when he discovers the round head of the nail stuck in between the tread groove. The silver metal bounces off the light of the flashlight.

"Here's the problem," the officer points at the nail.

Torres walks over to the tire to see what the offiicer had found and got a sick feeling at what he saw. If this happened any other night, Torres would have dismissed it as he simply ran over a nail, but something about this did not feel right. Too many things were all happening at once for this to be a coincidence. ***The missing spare tire, even if Agali had one and use it already doesn't explain why he would remove the jack.*** The officer steps away from Torres and continues walking around the vehicle, flashing his light through the car's windows. Torres stood there, staring at the tire trying to put the pieces of that night together. ***If Agali did deliberately do this... why? Why would he do this to his own car? Trying to get rid of me maybe, it would explain why he was so willing to lend me his car.*** Now Torres was starting to believe Agali has something to do with Christina's behavior. ***He must have put drugs in her food when he brought out prepared plates.*** Torres remembered how Christina complained about how she wasn't feeling well earlier yesterday morning. ***I need to get home.***

"Were you comin' from?" [Where are you coming from]

The officer asked, interrupting Torres' train of thought.

"Huh," Torres had a hard time understanding the sheriff's strong southern accent.

"I say, were you comin' from?"

"Oh, um, home, I'm coming from my house."

"Were you headed dis time of nigh'?" [where are you going at this time of night]

"I have a personal family emergency. Look, officer, I'm in a hurry to get back home now. I think after the flat tire, I should go home and call my friend in the morning."

A fear rose in Torres, he decided instead of going to Josh's house he needs to get back home to Christina as soon as possible. The thought of her being alone where Agali can get to her made him very anxious.

"Were yo' spare?" [where's your spare] The Officer asked.

"I don't have one."

"You called somebody?"

"No, I forgot my phone at home."

"Let me see your licenses and registration."

"I don't have my wallet either officer and this isn't my car."

Torres quickly turned his pockets inside out to show he didn't have anything, but the keys to his car and home, and Agali's spare car keys.

"I have one I just forgot it at home."

Torres nervously waited for the officer's response. The officer thought for a moment. He thought it was a strange time to be going to a friend's house, but there wasn't any evidence of Torres doing anything illegal. He didn't look as if he was hiding something or under the influence. Torres was noticeably tired and looked worried. The officer realized when he wasn't asking Torres questions, Torres would stare off in space, he showed he had a lot on his mind. The officer continues to analyze the situation. He looked Torres up and down. All Torres was wearing were army cargo pants, no shirt, and bare feet. ***He musta [must have] left the house fast, cause he ain't take nothing with him.*** The sheriff instructed Torres to close the trunk. Stand facing in front of the flat tire with his hands on the vehicle. He went back to his police cruiser and ran the plates to see if the car was stolen. When the plates showed a clear record, he then went back to Torres, got his information, and wrote him a ticket for not having his license on him. He called a 24-hour towing service for him and left once the tow truck arrived.

"How you doing?"

The tow truck driver greeted, holding his hand out to shake. He, too, had a strong southern accent. He was Caucasian as well, but younger. He looked like he couldn't have been more than 24 years old, he was slim and about an inch shorter than Torres. Torres sighs,

"I could be a lot better," Torres responded to his greeting and shook his hand.

"The officer said you gotta flat tire?"

"Yeah,"

Torres pointed down at the rear tire. The young tow truck driver went into his pants pocket to get out his phone and clicked on its flashlight.

"Oh, I can plug that up for ya [you] and have ya [you] on yo [your] way."

"That would be great, but how much do you charge?"

Torres's feeling of relief quickly faded when he realizes he doesn't have any money.

"$20."

"Do you accept debit cards?"

"Yes, sir."

"Ok, one more question, can you type the card number in if I don't physically have the card on me?"

"Yeah, I should be able to."

"YES, ok."

"Alright, you want it plugged?" The young tow truck driver asked to be sure.

"Yes, please."

The young tow truck driver went back to his truck to get his tire plug kit and his jack. Torres walked over to the driver's side and pressed his back to the car door. While the tow truck driver worked on the tire, Torres begins to stress trying to remember either his or Christina's debit card number and his mind continue to draw a blank. He finally gave up and thought the best thing for him to do is come up with a plan B.

"Excuse me, sir, can I use your phone to make a quick call,

please?"

Torres thought to call Josh and ask him to pay for the tire plug.

"Yeah, sure."

The young tow truck driver nicely gave Torres his phone with no hesitation. Torres glanced at the time display at the top right corner of the tow truck driver's phone. It was now 2:48 am.

"Josh's going to be pissed, I'm calling him at this time,"

Torres mumbled. He dialed Josh's number and let it ring. The phone rang five times, then went to voicemail. Torres called back again, and the same thing happens.

"Come on, Josh, man, pick up the phone." Torres mutter.

As time went by, Torres called Josh seven times, and all his calls unanswered. He was starting to panic again. The tow truck driver almost finished repairing the tire, and right now, he has no way to pay him. Torres called one more time and again no answer. The tow truck driver finished putting the tire back on and was now letting the car down off the jack.

"You're all set, sir."

Torres swallowed hard. He was so worried he had started sweating. Since Josh didn't answer the phone, he thought maybe he could convince the driver to follow him back to his house. The young tow truck driver had gathered all his tools and jack and loaded it into the truck.

"You can come on over to the truck, sir, and I'll take yo [your] card number."

"Oh fuck," Torres moaned.

He slowly made his way to the tow truck. The tow truck driver invited him to sit on the passenger side while he grabs the company's iPad. Torres gets in and watches as the young tow truck driver gets all set up. He begins to pull up the screen that allows him to type the credit card information manually.

"Ok, ready."

He looks up from the screen at Torres.

"Ummm..."

Torres was at a loss for words. Just then, the phone rings. It was Josh returning the missed calls. Torres looks down at the phone, shocked. He had forgotten he still had the tow truck driver's phone.

"It's my friend...Hello!" He quickly answered.

"Who's this?" Josh asked, sounding groggy as if he had just woken up.

"Josh, Josh, it's me, Torres. Listen, I need you to give me your credit card number so I can pay this tow truck driver."

"What? Tow truck driver? Where are you?" Josh asked. He was confused about what Torres was asking him.

"Josh, please, I will explain everything to you later. I need it now can you give me the number please."

"Hold on,"

Josh grunted, annoy to be awoken this time of night, and having somebody ask him for money all at the same time. About a minute later, Josh returns with his debit card in his hand, ready to call out the numbers. Torres gave the phone to the tow truck driver. He took Josh's information and asked for Torres to sign for him. The tow truck driver handed his phone back to Torres so he could say goodbye to his friend. Torres thanked Josh and promised he would explain everything in the morning.

"Thank you, man," Torres said to the young tow truck driver holding his hand out to shake.

"No problem. You enjoy the rest of yo morning; get home safe."

"Thanks, you too."

Torres exits the tow truck and jogs back to the SUV. With the flat tire incident being over, he still couldn't be at ease because there was a problem ahead of him with Christina. Torres has a strong feeling Agali is up to something, and he needs to hurry back to her. He planned to check on her, and if she were abnormal, he would seek medical help. Then Torres plans to confront Agali and get the truth behind all the chaos. He pulled back on the highway and continues to his exit to turn around and get interstate 526 west to head back towards his home.

Chapter Twenty

Exhausted from trying to gain control of Christina and from lack of sleep, Agali rubs the side of his neck and shoulder, trying to relieve the tightness in his muscles he was feeling caused by the stress of it all. He had a long night that was soon turning into the early morning. Agali thought he had accomplished everything he needed to get done up to this point. He has Christina, Torres is away dealing with a flat tire, and with Madam Jay's help, he will finally have what he has wanted since he met Christina. A wife. Agali looked over to Madam Jay, who stood there staring at Christina.

"Are you ready?" He asked.

Madam Jay heard Agali's voice but didn't understand his question because her mind was fully focused on Christina. She broke her gaze and turned to acknowledge him.

"Are you ready?" He repeated.

Madam Jay nodded her head, "yes."

"I'm going out back to get some rope, let's set everything up in the dining room."

After his instructions, Agali leaves the room and heads outside. Madam Jay watched Agali as he left the room then starts to walk towards the stairs, needing to go to the bedroom to retrieve her burlap sack, but before she moves out of the living room, she takes one last look at Christina. Who laid lifeless on the sofa, it was like she was unconscious, or maybe even dead? Madam Jay found herself staring at Christina again, she was afraid to go near her, but was curious to know was Christina still alive. Her curiosity got the best of her as she turns around and starts walking back towards Christina. As Madam Jay stood over her, she noticed that she didn't even see the rising and falling in Christina's chest to indicate she was breathing. Madam Jay reached down to touch the side of Christina's neck to check for a pulse. She found one, and Christina's heart pumped rapidly as it did before when Agali checked it. Before she could react to the abnormal pulse, she felt a cool breeze blow behind her and what felt like a tap on her shoulder. Madam Jay gulped as she quickly turned around and looked but saw nothing nor no one. She dismissed it as maybe the breeze was caused by Agali leaving a window open in another room in the house, and the tap on the shoulder, well Madam Jay just ignored, since she couldn't explain it. Thinking she just imagined it since her nerves are on edge. Taking a deep breath then exhaling it, she glances back to Christina.

"Whoa!"

Madam Jay yells out, trips, and falls back onto the coffee table. When Madam Jay looked back to Christina, her blood-red eyes were wide open, and she had a creepy grin on her face with a mouthful of pointed razor-sharp teeth. It was like looking at the mouth of a shark. When Madam Jay falls on the coffee table, at that moment, she manages to look away from Christina. When she looks at Christina again, the smile is gone, and her eyes were closed. It was over just as quick as it happened, and Christina laid there back in a lifeless state. Madam Jay gasped for air, inhaling and exhaling, trying to calm down. Hoping that maybe she didn't see what she thought she saw, perhaps lack of rest was causing her to see things. Madam Jay again blamed imagination. All she knew was she wanted this to be over. She lifts herself from the coffee table. Her small light body caused no damage to it. She rushed out of the living room and went upstairs without looking back.

Agali enters through the back door, walking through the kitchen, carrying ten feet of rope thrown over his shoulder. He goes over to the kitchen drawer next to the stove, his "junk drawer," and grabs his multi-functional stainless-steel scissors. He cuts the rope in pieces, each about two feet long. When he finished, he had five pieces of rope. Since he only needed four pieces for Christina's arms and legs. He put the extra piece of rope and scissors back into the "junk drawer," then headed towards the dining room. As he walked through the opened entryway that connected the dining room to the living room, he saw Madam Jay hasn't yet gotten the dining room ready. Annoyed, he then took a chair from the dining table and placed it far from the dining table, sitting it off by itself and having nothing close by around it. The chair is an old-fashioned armchair, brown wood stain with a white cushioned seat. Agali laid his pieces of rope on the floor in front of the chair then walks into the living room to get Christina. The closer he got to her, the more excited he became. ***It's almost over, and she's soon going to be mine***. He thought as a smile widens on his face. Agali bent down and scooped Christina up in his arms. Still, in her lifeless looking state, her head and left arm dangled as Agali carries her to the dining room. Madam Jay walks into the dining room at the same time Agali enters in with Christina. He gives her an irritated look but says nothing. Agali gently seats Christina in the chair and begins tying her arms and legs onto it. Once he finished, Christina sat bond to the chair with her head hung low and her shoulders slumped. Agali backed away from Christina, allowing Madam Jay to do her part.

First, Madam Jay grabbed a plastic bag from the burlap sack that contains a mixture of dirt (that Agali got for her from the Sosa's property) and ashes. She begins dumping it out, a little bit at a time until she had completed a closed circle around Christina. Next, on the inner layer of the circle, she pours salt down all the way around in a closed circle. Madam Jay takes out four large, wide, and white candles, then arranges them in an "X" shape on the floor in front of the circles she has surrounding Christina. Putting the candles diagonally from one another as the ends of an "X." Using more salt to make lines to connect them. She lights them. At that moment, Madam Jay takes out of her burlap sack, a dried wing of a black hen, a chicken foot, and a mojo bag. The chicken foot will make light scratches on Christina, to scratch off all the negative energy that is on her. The idea behind it would remind you of someone using a facial scrub brush to exfoliate the dead skin. The wing of a black hen brushes off the expose negative energy, and mojo bags are traditionally used to draw luck or love, but in some cases, they can be used for other things. Madam Jay fixed this mojo bag earlier for this ritual; to help her to rid these evil entities. Madam Jay steps inside the circle she made and placed the mojo bag on Christina's lap, thinking it would be more affected with direct contact. Agali stood quietly outside the circles anxiously waiting for this to be over and hoping that it works. Madam Jay steps back out of the circles and grabs her burlap sack to take out the last item inside. Her King James bible. She already had a piece of paper holding the scripture she wanted. It was the book of Psalms…chapter twenty-three. Madam Jay took a deep breath, clears her throat, and begins.

"De Lawd, É duh my sheppud. Uh een gwoi' want. É…" [The Lord is my shepherd; I shall not want. He…]

"Wait, hush," Agali interrupted.

Madam Jay immediately stopped and listened. Agali stood puzzled as he listened to every single door in the house, the closets, bedrooms, bathroom, front and back door even the swing door to the kitchen begin to open. They could hear doorknobs turning, and the hinges squeaking as the doors widen. The sound stopped, and it was silent again. All the light bulbs in the house burst simultaneously. The dining room darkens. Both Agali and Madam Jay look at each other. Then at the exact same time, all the doors slams shut all at once. This time Madam Jay hollers at the sudden loud slams. Agali jumped and was rattled. Both of their hearts raced. Madam Jay started to tremble. The bible she was still holding, slams closed in her hands then drops to the floor. It then slides across the floor on its own and leaves out of the dining room. The mojo bag on Christina's lap starts to vibrate, yet Christina hadn't moved. The mojo bag shook for a moment, Madam Jay and Agali just stood and watched. The mojo bag stops shaking…rolls off Christina's lap and onto the floor, then burst into flames.

"WHAT'S HAPPENING?!"

Agali yelled, grabbing Madam Jay by her arms. Madam Jay just shook her head from side to side, too afraid to speak; she couldn't get out the words "I don't know." Agali was starting to panic himself.

"Well, do something, finish this?!" He ordered.

Suddenly, disembodied whispers filled the room. They were

loud enough to hear but unintelligible to make out what was being said. Christina begins to moan, but this time her moans aren't from pain, but of pleasure. She sits up straight in the chair and rotates her head in a slow-motion circle. She muffled a chuckle or more like a scoff. Agali lets Madam Jay go, and turns his attention to Christina, her pleasurable moans, were like music to his ears. Agali finds himself getting lost into the sound, he wanted to be near her, to touch her, but as soon as he fully planted his right foot inside the circles, Madam Jay had made. Christina's eyes pop open, exposing her red glowing eyes. Light illuminates from her eyes. She chuckles, but her laugh changes from the sound of her voice to a deep voice.

"Thy shalt not covet thy neighbor's wife." She mocked.

The voice that came out of her echoed like she was roaring and talking at the same time. Agali stepped back out of the circle. His eyes widen, he was shocked and horrified, but before he could even react to what he just heard, Christina started laughing again. She cackles uncontrollably, her body jerks and bounces like she's having a seizure. Madam Jay felt something wet touch her top lip, she reaches and touches the liquid on her face. She used the burning light from the candles to see. It was blood. Her nose was bleeding. She gasped.

"Leggo, É cyan' help um." [Let's go, I can't help her]

Before Agali could express his disappointment, Christina screeches. Both Madam Jay and Agali cowards to the floor with a finger in both ears, trying to dull the sound. Seeing Madam Jay's help was useless, Agali feels his only chance was to make a run for it. He figured the circles Madam Jay had surrounding Christina would hold her long enough for him to escape out of the house.

Even though all the lights were out, and the only light came from the candles and Christina's glowing eyes. Agali knew his home like the back of his hand. He surely knew his way out of the dining room to the front door without the help of any light. He was going to go for it, but as soon as he stood to his feet, Christina's screams cease immediately. She glares at Agali with those glowing red eyes piercing through his soul. He starts taking deep gasps like he was hyperventilating; his heart was in his throat. Christina didn't blink. She keeps her evil glare on him.

Again, Agali felt that the circles that surround her would keep her in place. He builds up enough courage to move, but as soon as he jerked to run, as soon as he lifts his right foot, his right foot did a 180-degree turn on its own, breaking his ankle. Agali heard the loud snap his ankle made when it broke. He falls to the floor, crying out in pain. Christina growls, she jumps to her feet, breaking the chair to pieces in the process. It was like the chair exploded, sending pieces flying across the room. Christina took steps towards them. She walks to the edge of the circle then stops. Madam Jay passes out. Agali sits on the floor, trying to breathe through both the pain from his ankle and his fear. Christina takes another step. She steps directly on top of the salt, dirt, and ashes, sliding her foot back and forth as her way to taunt Agali, that his little protection circles were no match for the beast inside her. The candles blow out. Now the only light in the dark house is coming from Christina's glowing eyes. Agali could see a dark silhouette of her body and her eyes. Agali hoped that the neighbors heard Christina's screams and had called the police. He laid on the floor and watched how Christina's eyes glared at him from five feet away to hovering over him in mere seconds. Agali crawls, using his arms and good leg to hurry across the floor. Breathing hard and sweating as if he was on his feet running. He manages to make it to the front door, he reaches for the doorknob, but before he has a chance to grab it. Christina appears behind him and starts dragging him by his broken ankle back into the dining room.

"OH GOD, NOOOOO…HELP!" Agali cries.

Chapter Twenty-One

Torres took his chances going eighty miles per hour back to Agali's, he had already gotten a ticket and a warning from the sheriff, and if he were to get pulled over now, he would be in big trouble. Despite this, Torres couldn't focus on anything, but getting back to his wife as soon as possible, regretting leaving in the first place, he allowed his fear to overpower his good judgment. It seems his luck changed for the better as he reaches his neighborhood without incident. Torres made a quick turn into Agali's driveway, almost hitting the mailbox in the process. He was exhausted, but the adrenaline running through him gave him the energy he needed to keep going. Torres jumped out of the SUV and ran to the front door. He noticed all the lights in Agali's house were out. He figured Agali and his friend had already gone to bed but didn't care and proceeded to bang on the front door. He felt like this whole night was Agali's fault, and he needed answers. Torres barely got any sleep, so he wasn't going to let Agali nor his friend get any sleep either. Torres banged on the door harder; in a rage, he was about to start kicking the door until he realized he wasn't wearing shoes. He caught himself before his foot hit the door. Irritated, Torres continued to pound the door for ten minutes. He knocked and banged on the door so hard that a neighbor on the other side of Agali's house heard the noise. A light came on upstairs in one of the neighbor's rooms, followed by the lifting and bending in the mini blinds in one of the downstairs windows. He watched the house for a second to see if someone was going to come out on the porch. When a moment past and nothing more happened, he felt he should keep the noise down some before one of the neighbors decides to call the police but he wasn't going to give up that easy. Torres decided to go around the house and try knocking on the back door.

"When I came over the first time, it didn't take Agali long at all to answer. He better wake up." Torres grumbled.

Torres was extremely upset at this point, and he was ready to punch Agali in the face. He sprinted towards the back yard. Torres made it halfway around the house before stopping dead in his tracks. His jaw dropped when he saw Christina; sitting on the ground right in the middle where his and Agali's yards joined.

Torres was immediately unnerved by the sight of her but knew he needed to do something. He slowly crept toward her. The closer he got, the better he could see her. Christina was sitting on her knees with her back facing him, and her head thrown back, facing towards the sky. She repeatedly slammed the sides of her fists down on the ground in a rhythmic motion. Torres could hear her chanting but couldn't make out what Christina was saying. He would have dismissed it as gibberish, but he notices how she chanted the words with authority as if whatever she was saying had meaning behind it, and her chants flowed with the rhythm of her pounding. His blood ran cold when Christina's voice changes into a deep distorted man's voice. It was not as if she was making her voice deep herself, but the voice that came from her sounded clear and natural. ***That's not Christina***. He thought. He was starting to doubt it was her, but as he got closer, there was no question whether it was Christina or not. As he felt himself drawing closer to her, he could see it was truly his wife, she was still wearing the same white midi dress she wore to the therapy session, but now the dress is almost unrecognizable, the white color of the dress was no longer visible.

Instead, the entire dress was brown and dingy like it was water stained. There were also dark black spots on Christina's back and around her shoulders. Torres stood beside her and watched her. She continued to chant and slam her fists to the ground.

"Christina?" Torres called.

She didn't respond.

"Baby?"

He reached out and rested his hand on Christina's shoulder. The moment he touched her, she immediately stopped chanting and slamming her fist. She dropped her head down and sat completely still, and all was quiet. The only sound heard was Torres's heavy breathing, as anxiety rushed through him.

"Christina?"

Soon after he releases her shoulder, a scream bursts from Christina like the blare of a fire alarm after it detects smoke. She screams at the top of her lungs. The sudden outburst causes Torres to fall backward to the ground. The shock from it all knocked him off his feet. Christina's screams only lasted a few seconds until she abruptly stopped, then passes out. Torres' heart pounded as he gasped for breath. He was surprised he didn't have a heart attack. He took a moment to gather himself before crawling over to her. He placed his hand on her again, but this time nothing happens. He looked around to see if anyone had heard her screams and came outside to see what was wrong. To his surprise, no one was around, but that didn't guarantee no one heard her. How could they not have heard a woman's high-pitched scream, in a quiet neighborhood at now 4:30 am? Torres knew he needed to get Christina to a doctor and decided to wait on confronting Agali. He realized he hadn't given Agali his car keys back yet, so he figured since Agali is not answering his door. He could use Agali's car again to take Christina to the hospital. He stood to his feet, then scooped Christina up in his arms, he paused for a second to see if moving Christina woke her, but it didn't. She was unconscious. He knew there was no time to waste, but he wanted to go home first, get dressed, and grab his wallet and phone. When Torres enters his front door with Christina, he too was hit with the same horrible smell of rotting meat Agali and Madam Jay encounter before.

"Oh man, what the fuck!" Torres gagged.

He had no time to dwell on or look for the source of the smell. He needed to hurry up and get Christina to a hospital. He gently laid Christina on the sofa, then darted upstairs to their bedroom. He threw on a t-shirt, and his tennis shoes then snatched his phone and wallet off his nightstand. He hurried back downstairs, grabbed Christina, and rushed out the door.

When Torres arrived at the hospital, he quickly received the help he needed. A nurse was standing behind the desk, talking to the medical assistant, she saw Torres carrying Christina in and immediately called for a gurney. Torres watched as the medical team took Christina away to examine her. The assistant politely motioned him over to her to hand him some papers to fill out. Torres took the papers, then collapsed into a chair in the waiting room, and just took a moment to breathe. He felt now that he is at the hospital, the doctors could tell him exactly what was wrong and what to do, and things would go back to normal. Torres couldn't fight the gut feeling he had that Agali did something to Christina. If the doctor comes back and tells him that there were drugs in her system, he will immediately contact the authorities and have Agali arrested. Torres felt because of Christina's behavior, she had to be under the influence of something, and everything that he saw and that had happened had a rational explanation to it. Even though he wasn't sure what that explanation was, he wasn't going to let irrational thoughts flood his mind. He started on the paperwork the assistant had given him and stumble with it. When he got to the part that asked "the reason for the visit" all he could think to put was his wife had been acting strange, she mentioned of feeling nauseous, and her eyes were discolored, then added narcotics are the likely reason for her change in mental state and symptoms. He had only hoped he wasn't too late. He starts to beat himself up about why he just didn't dial 911 when the incident first occurred at midnight. Instead, he cowardly ran out of the house. It's hard enough for a man to handle a cowardly move, but it's even harder for a soldier. Torres felt if something happens to Christina, he could never forgive himself. Even though Agali was the cause, he took the blame also for leaving her alone.

Torres gave an exhausted sigh and continued finishing the paperwork. When he got to the signature and date, he realized he had forgotten the date. Torres took his phone out to see what it was, and that's when he saw he had five missed calls and two voicemails. He didn't recognize the number, so he called his voicemail to listen to the messages.

The voicemail prompt begins, then a woman's voice, "Hello, I'm trying to get in touch with Mr. Torres Sosa, I'm Amy Simpson, I am the co-ordinator of Loving Hearts, and I need to talk to you in regarding Dr. Christina Sosa. Could you please get back to me as soon as possible?" The voicemail prompt plays again and then another message, "This is Amy Simpson again, please call me back. Christina left the session hysterical. I was concerned, so I went to her home...*Amy's voice gets shaky. She starts to cry. Amid her tears, she manages to get out...* "Is Christina ok?" And with that, the call ends. A chill ran down Torres' spine, and nervousness filled him again. ***What did she mean by Christina left the session hysterical?*** He wondered. Torres was starting to grasp the fact that he wasn't the only one who witnessed Christina's strange behavior.

He saw it was almost 6:00 am and debated whether to call Amy so early. After thinking it over, he decided it would be best to wait. He handed the paperwork to the medical assistant, who assured him someone would let him know Christina's condition as soon as possible. He took his seat back in the waiting room and tried his best to relax. Ten minutes later, Torres watched as people enter in and out the electric hospital's doors. Watching those individuals entering and exiting was like counting sheep. The adrenaline was gone, and now his body has relaxed. The missed hours of sleep caught up with him when he finds himself getting drowsy. He felt someone shaking his right arm, and it awoke him, he turned to see who interrupted his nap. He glances right and immediately closes his eyes and rubs them surprise by what he saw. He stopped rubbing his eyes and tried to focus them when he was sure he saw clearly; Torres looks back to make sure his eyes weren't deceiving him.

"Christina...what are you doing here? Are you alright?" Torres asked, stunned at the sight of her.

Christina sat in the waiting room, sitting next to him, looking completely normal for the first time since the dinner with Agali.

"Hey, honey, what's up?" She asked nonchalantly.

She sat with her legs crossed, sitting in her chair sideways, facing his direction. Torres continued to stare in disbelief. Christina smiled and began to hike her dress up and gave Torres a seductive look.

"Christina, are you ok, what did the doctor say?"

Torres asked, slightly disturbed at what he saw. Nothing about Christina was attractive at that moment. She was still dirty with matted hair, and that midi dress she's wearing should be in the trash.

"I'm fine, baby."

She grinned, blowing kisses at him, and licking her lips, still trying to seduce him. She uncrossed her legs and leaned forward towards him, and Torres leaned back. She smiled wider and stared at him, looking as if she just escaped from the insane asylum.

"Kiss me!" She demanded.

"No, baby, something is still wrong with you, I'm calling the nurse."

Torres stood and headed towards the medical assistant, but before he could get near her, Christina snarls, Torres quickly turns around and looks at her. Christina was on her hands and knees growling at him, showing the same razor-sharp teeth, Madam Jay saw earlier. He slowly takes steps back away from her. Torres was scared but refused to run this time. He made up in his mind he is going to get his wife the help she needed. Christina crawled a little towards him, still snarling. Torres' breathing quickens. He glares at her watching her every movement as she crawled on the floor, pacing back and forth without taking her eyes off him. She stops. It was a standoff between the two. He thought to grab her and get her back to the doctors to be examined. Amazed, Christina got away from the ER without anyone noticing. ***She needs some help, and there's no way they would have discharged her with this behavior. She must have escaped.*** He thought. He decided to take hold of her and drag her back to the ER examining area, but before he could react, Christina charges at him and bites down on his neck, chewing on his main artery. Torres didn't know what he was more shocked by the pain or the fact that his wife bit him. He yells and fights to get Christina off him.

"STOP, ST…he starts to choke on his own blood.

Torres bounced and kicked in his seat, grunting loudly, grabbing at his throat.

"SIR…SIR?!" The nurse called. "SIR, WAKE UP!"

The nurse shook Torres by the shoulder, trying to wake him from his nightmare.

"GET OFF ME!"

He yelled as he pushes the nurse's hand off his shoulder.

"Sir, are you okay!"

The nurse ignored his shove and grabbed him by both shoulders. Torres opened his eyes and looked all around him. He fights to breathe like he had just came up out of water.

"Look at me…are you okay?" the nurse asked firmly.

Torres looks up at the nurse then back around him. He saw all the confused stares on the people's faces who sat in the waiting room and the look of concern from the medical assistant. The nurse gripped his face.

"Hey, look at me, are you okay." The nurse asked again.

"Yeah, yeah, I'm fine. Bad dream." Torres finally answers.

The nurse sighs. "Come with me please, the doctor would like to talk to you about your wife."

Torres felt slightly embarrassed about the scene he caused. He was glad to leave the room at that moment as the people continued to stare. The nurse swiped her badge to open the door that leads to the back of the ER, then instructed him to wait there for the doctor. Five minutes past while Torres waited for the doctor. He was starting to regain his composure; he saw the medical assistant from the hallway he was standing in through an open doorway where she was seated at her desk. Torres notices her constant looks over her shoulder at him. He could tell she was a little worried about him. He gave her a quick wave and smile to assure he was fine now. The message of "*I'm good now, stop looking at me like I'm crazy*" was well received. She smiled back at him then turns back to her computer.

"Mr. Sosa!"

The doctor called as he approached Torres from behind. Torres was shocked by how that startled him. He is not an anxious person at all, but all that has happened was starting to make him a little jumpy.

"Hi, I'm Dr. Foreman," he extended his hand to shake.

He was the same height and billed as Torres. Torres looked him directly in his blue eyes and thought to himself. ***This guy can't be any older than 30; he must be fresh out of Medical School.***

"I examined your wife," he said while looking at her charts.

"And um…" The doctor paused as he continued reading.

His pause causes Torres to brace himself for the bad news.

"She's fine, what was your reason for bringing her in?" Torres couldn't believe what he was hearing.

"What?" He finally asked.

"Yeah, other than the fact she was a bit dirty, medically, she's fine. All her vitals were normal; she was negative for all the standard tests. I saw where you wrote about, she uses drugs…"

"No," Torres interrupted. "I meant she might have been drugged."

"Meaning?" The doctor questioned, wanting to clarify what Torres was telling him.

"I mean, we went to somebody's house for dinner, and she hasn't been the same since."

"Have you gone to the Authorities?"

"Look, I don't know for sure if she was drugged, as for now it's only an assumption, that's why I brought her here for you guys to test her and get me proof."

"Well, if there were drugs in her system, those test results won't be in until tomorrow."

"What do you mean, she's fine?"

Torres was still finding it hard to comprehend that despite everything that has happened with Christina she's fine.

"Come, let's go see your wife."

Dr. Foreman led him around the corner and into a large room full of beds lined up against the walls, in little boxed sections with only curtains separating them. They approached a section on the left side of the room. In the boxed section they were walking towards, Torres saw the shadow of a person standing near the opening of the curtain. The curtain swiftly opens, showing the one who was inside. It was the same nurse who had woke Torres from the bad dream he had in the waiting room. She smiled at him, followed by a quick nod as her way of being polite, but didn't stop to talk. She continued pass, and Dr. Foreman pulls back the curtain allowing Torres to enter first.

"Honey! I'm so happy to see you!" Christina exclaimed.

He was amazed at what he saw. Christina looked like she was back to her old self. An aid gave Christina a bed bath when she first arrived at the hospital while she was still unconscious. After the medical team looked over Christina and saw she was stable, they couldn't figure out why or how she became unconscious. There was no head swelling or any indication that she had a head injury. There were no signs of a seizure, no signs of a stroke; her blood pressure and blood sugar level were all normal. There weren't any medical reasons, they could find to explain Christina being healthy yet unresponsive. It was diagnosis that she was dehydrated and collapsed from exhaustion. Torres stared at her for a moment,

"Her eyes are still red!" He proclaimed.

"Waking from a deep sleep can cause slight discoloration to a person's eyes."

Dr. Foreman responded. Slowly, Torres walked to the foot of the hospital bed, still trying to process the situation.

"What happened, why am I here, and why are you looking at me like that?" Christina questioned.

Torres couldn't answer at that moment; he was so stunned that all he could do was shake his head.

"How are you feeling?" Dr. Foreman chimed in.

"I feel fine," Christina replied.

"And as far as your test results show, you are fine."

Dr. Foreman remarked. He stood beside the hospital bed, checking the monitors making sure her vitals were still strong. Then shook his head, confirming he was right. Dr. Foreman and Christina both looked at Torres, awaiting an answer.

"You can't be serious!" Torres shouted. "Christina, don't you remember complaining about feeling sick yesterday morning? What about last night when you yelled at me then started slithering across the floor?"

As Torres flooded Christina with questions, both her and Dr. Foreman just stared at him.

"She slithered across the floor?" Dr. Foreman asked, wrinkling his brow, trying to understand what Torres meant by that.

"Yeah, like a snake!" Torres yelled.

"Christina, do you remember any of this?" Dr. Foreman asked. Christina shook her head "no," almost as if she was afraid to answer. They return their gaze to Torres, looking at him like he was a mad man.

"I have another question, where were you this past week?" Dr. Foreman asked Christina.

"I was home; I wasn't out of town or anything." She responded.

"Do you usually wear the same clothes for days in a row?" He added.

"She has only had that dress on for one day; she put it on yesterday," Torres answered for her.

"Yesterday?" Dr. Foreman asked, stunned by how dirty the dress was, to only have been worn one day.

"How did she get so dirty?" He looked at Torres.

"I don't know she was like that when I found her in the back yard. Christina, you were chanting something. What was it?" Torres asked.

Christina shook her head and shrugged. She doesn't remember being in the back yard.

"Christina, you don't remember anything?"

Torres was starting to get upset. Christina was the one with the problem, yet he's the one who seems crazy.

"No, honey, I don't." She answered, trying to hold back tears. Torres was beginning to scare her.

"What about Amy Simpson, she called me several times asking about you. She thinks something is wrong with you as well."

Christina broke her gaze from Torres. She tosses her feet to the floor on the other side of the bed, turning her back toward Dr. Foreman. Amy's name triggers a flashback. Torres noticed her reaction. He took a step closer to her but said nothing more, allowing her to gather her thoughts.

"Amy…the therapy session." She whispered.

"What is it babe, what do you remember?"

"I…I was walking and was afraid. I blacked out and…Uh…" she grunted.

Trying to recall that memory of what happened was giving her a headache.

"I can't remember." She groans from the pain in her head.

"If you want, I could schedule a psych evaluation."

Dr. Foreman suggested. They both were almost startled by the sound of his voice. With Christina trying to remember and Torres' focus was on her. They forgot for a second that the doctor was still there. Hearing the doctor's suggestion made Christina's stomach turn, she didn't want to respond and thought it would be best for Torres to decide.

"Am I that bad?" she asked him.

Torres saw the pain in his wife's eyes and the worried look,on her face. He let out an exaggerated sigh then turns towards the doctor.

"Is she healthy enough to go home, doctor?"

"Physically, yes." Dr. Foreman's reply was almost sarcastic.

"Then we are just going to go home and get some rest we both had a long night," Torres said in a defeated tone.

Chapter Twenty-Two

As they rode home, Torres took a moment to explain how he ended up driving Agali's car, then questions the whereabouts of his truck. His question, however, triggered something in Christina's mind that causes another flashback,

She could see herself standing in front of the entrance of the Loving Hearts Center, where the therapy session was held. She was confused and felt weary. She also realized she wasn't carrying anything. Which was unusual for her because she always brought something, even if it was just a wristlet. She had forgotten her purse inside, but she didn't want to go back in to get it. She then remembered the frightening experience she had that caused such a scene. Embarrassed, she knew she couldn't go back inside. She stood there for a moment, gathering her thoughts. Finally, taking her first steps, she felt the warmth of the sidewalk underneath her feet and realized she also left her shoes behind. ***Damn, what a day***. She thought. She looked around the parking lot, then back at the entrance door. She was alone. She contemplated for a moment on whether to go back in or just go home, before leaving her stuff behind.

Torres glances over at Christina, still awaiting an answer. He saw her staring straight ahead; it was clear she was lost in thought.

"Baby, did you hear me? What happened to my truck?"

He repeated, interrupting Christina's flashback.

"I left it at the center." Christina finally answered.

"Why, it could be towed away by now." Torres angrily stated.

"Honey, please, I don't remember why." She lied. "I just… something happened, and I left my purse there with the car keys in it and…" She let out a dramatic sigh. "If it did get towed, I'll pay for it, okay."

"That's not the point, so how did you get home?"

"Walked, I guess."

"You WALKED all the way home?!" Torres exclaimed in disbelief.

"YES, Torres!" Christina yelled back.

At least that's the last thing she remembers. The truth is Christina couldn't remember getting home. Her only memory is going towards a church then waking up in the hospital. Trying to remember what happened in between, gave her a massive headache.

"You didn't have your stuff, why'd you leave your purse?"

"Torres!" Christina whined. "You will get your truck back."

"Why didn't you call me?" He continued questioning her.

"No phone, Torres, I'm sorry about your truck, but I don't want to talk about this anymore. I told you what I remembered."

Torres sucked his teeth and shook his head.

"Ugh, my head is killing me, feels like someone hit me with a baseball bat." Christina groaned.

"You know I think Agali drugged us." Torres blurted out. "Because after we went to his house is when all this crazy shit started. I been hallucinating and having weird dreams, and you been acting strangely. If those test results come back saying drugs, I'm going to beat his ass and have him arrested."

"Wait a minute, weird dreams?" Christina recalled another memory, her reoccurring nightmares of the beast.

"Yeah, the dream was stupid and not even worth talking about." He sighed.

Torres gave her a look but didn't comment. He wondered how after everything he said about Agali drugging them, his dream was the only thing that stuck out to her. Christina wished Torres would have elaborated more instead of just brushing his dream off like it was nothing. ***Did he see it too?*** She wondered. Her thoughts begin to focus more and more on the beast. Christina's headaches grew worse as the image of the beast appears so vivid in her mind. The road in front of her and all her surroundings blacked out. All she could see was the image in her head. It was like she suddenly fell asleep and started dreaming. There it was, right in front of her, the beast. It had its back towards her, crouching on all fours. Its once long shiny black hair covering its body is now dull from being soaked in blood. She wanted to shake the image or look away but couldn't. It was like she had no control over her mind. So, she watches as blood drips off its body leaving a small puddle around it. The beast snatches its head around and looks directly at her, exposing its glowing red eyes. Christina shivers. The look in its eyes was so intense.

"Hey, what's wrong?"

Torres asks when he saw she quickly became frightened. His voice snapped her out of the image, haunting her mind. Christina's sight returns, she takes in some deep breaths and whines from her pounding headache.

"Christina, you ok? Talk to me."

"Yeah, yeah, I'm fine. I just, I don't feel well."

She never got a chance to talk to him about her nightmare, and after her doctor suggesting a psych evaluation, she thought now definitely wasn't a good time to mention it.

"You think he drugged us?" She asked, continuing with their previous conversation.

"What other reason could it be?"

"But why?"

"Jealousy, I've seen how he looks at you."

"Gross, I don't want to think about that either."

Christina was disgusted by the thought of Agali and her together. She didn't find Agali to be attractive at all. Torres huffs, he was annoyed with Agali and the fact his truck may be towed away agitated him more. It took everything in him to keep calm because he didn't want to take his anger out on Christina. They pulled into Agali's driveway, Torres again banged on Agali's front door, and there was no response. He decided to give up for now and wait to see Christina's test results. To confirm she had drugs in her system so that he could pursue Agali further. He put Agali's car keys inside his mailbox and headed home. Torres opened all the windows downstairs, to air out that horrible smell that seems to linger in their home. Christina went upstairs to their bedroom to lie down. Torres just wanted to stretch out on the sofa and relax for a while. The silence in their home and the peacefulness of the quiet neighborhood was calming his nerves. Enjoying the tranquility, he was startled by the sudden loud ringing from his cell phone. He sat up straight and tossed his legs onto the floor, then snatches the cell phone off the coffee table. The number appearing on the screen was the same number who called him several times the day before. "Amy?" He says to himself.

"Hello?" He answers.

"Hello, Mr. Sosa?"

"Yes, this is he."

"Hi, I'm Amy Simpson, I work with your wife Christina, I've been trying to get ahold of you."

"Yeah, I got your messages. I was going to call you back later today."

Torres looks at his phone to check the time. It's now 8:35 am.

"Is Christina okay?"

Amy just got straight to the point of her call. She had been worrying about Christina all night.

"Yes, yes, Christina's fine now. I took her to the emergency room this morning, and now she seems to be back to her old self. She is upstairs taking a nap."

Amy exhales a sigh of relief.

"I have her things; I don't mind driving over to bring them to you."

"Yeah, I would appreciate that, but Amy, by any chance, did see the truck my wife drove in?"

"Truck? You mean the large navy-blue SUV?"

"Yeah, that's it."

"Yes, Christina left it at the center."

"I know she told me, but do you think it's still there like is it possible it could have been towed?"

"Oh no, it's fine, it's still there. I lease the property alone, and I would be the one who would have it towed, and I didn't."

"Great." Torres exhales his sigh of relief as well.

"I'm on my way now to bring Christina's things and will see you shortly."

"Ok, see you then."

About three minutes pass after his conversation with Amy ended, Torres hears a knock at the door.

"Damn, that was fast." He whispered to himself as he goes to answer it.

"Hey, what's going on?" Sarah, Josh's wife, asks as soon as the door opened.

"Oh, it's you," Torres replied.

"Yes, it's me, what I'm not welcome here anymore."

"Yeah, it's just I thought you were somebody else."

"Who?"

"Just somebody is coming over to bring me something."

"Ok, well, can I come in?"

"Yeah."

Torres steps back from the door and allows Sarah to enter.

"Y'all air conditioner's not working?" Sarah asked when she saw all the windows opened.

"Yeah, it works just wanted some fresh air."

"Oh, Josh wanted me to come over and see how y'all was doing."

"We're fine. I'm sorry for calling so late."

He reached into his back pants pocket, retrieving his wallet, and pulls out a twenty-dollar bill.

"Here's the twenty I owe him."

Sarah took it and continued asking more questions.

"He said you got a flat tire last night. Where were you headed so late, and where's your truck now?"

"It's a long story Sarah, and again I'm sorry for disturbing you guys with my drama, it won't happen again, but my truck's fine, I'm going to go pick it up later."

"Where's Christina?"

"She's upstairs taking a nap."

Sarah could see from Torres' vague responses, that he didn't want to give any more details than what he was offering. She shrugged off the weird vibe of it all and accepted his answers.

"Alright, just as long as everything is ok. I guess I'll get going."

"Everything is fine, thanks for you guys concern and I'll call Josh later."

"Of course, we are concern about y'all. You're like family, and have Christina call me when she wakes up."

"I will."

When Torres opens the door to let Sarah out, they both are surprised to see Amy in mid knocking motion, and the sudden opening of the door surprised her as well.

"Oh my!" Amy exclaimed.

"Hey, sorry, didn't hear you drive up, you must be Amy," Torres said.

He allowed Amy inside, and Sarah followed behind her.

"Oh goodness, it's okay, yes I'm Amy, nice to finally meet you, Mr. Sosa." She extended her hand to shake.

"Call me Torres, nice to meet you too."

"Hi, I'm Sarah, I'm Torres' best friend's wife."

Sarah chimed in, extending her hand, introducing herself to Amy, and Amy returned the greeting.

"Here are Christina's things. Amy handed Torres Christina's black tote bag along with her black high heel shoes of which she had placed inside of a plastic grocery bag.

"I know you told me she was sleeping but is there any possible way I could talk to her, just for a moment I've been worried sick," Amy pleaded.

Sarah turns to Torres, stunned by what she was hearing.

"What's wrong with Christina?" she asked.

Sarah and Christina have not known each other as long as Josh and Torres, but they developed a friendship through their brotherhood. Enough so that each will want to be informed if something happens to the other. Something Sarah thought Torres knew and felt insulted that he would keep that type of information from her.

"She was sick yesterday, but I took her to the doctor, and she's fine now," Torres explained.

"I still would like to see her." Amy protested.

"Why didn't you tell me this before?" Sarah questioned.

Soon everyone was all talking at once, but about a minute into the debate, Sarah abruptly stops arguing when something catches her attention.

"Wait, wait, be quiet." Sarah shushes. "Y'all hear that?"

They all listened. The sound they heard was of someone singing, and it came from upstairs.

"Christina must have turned on the radio," Torres said.

"That means she's awake!" Amy said in excitement.

"No listen, that's not the radio, there's no music, it's just the sound of someone singing," Sarah noted.

"It is the radio because there's no one up there, but Christina and that's not her voice," Torres argued.

Sarah started up the stairs with Torres and Amy following her close behind. The closer they got to the master bedroom, the louder and clearer the song got.

"Then she must have the radio on a Spanish station cause that's not English," Sarah added.

"Ok, I'm Hispanic, we listen to Spanish music sometimes."

Torres lied, despite the fact he is Puerto Rican, he was born and raised in New Jersey, and Spanish wasn't spoken much in his home. So, he couldn't speak fluent Spanish and only knew a few words of it. Not enough to understand a song in Spanish, and Christina didn't usually listen to anything but R&B. Despite this, he still convinced himself that it was only the radio they heard and was aggravated, Sarah was making it seem as if it was something else. The way they all crept towards the master's bedroom, and the gut feeling he was getting that something may be wrong, was upsetting him more. Torres had enough with all the weird things that were happening to them. They all stood in front of the master bedroom. The singing was even louder. They could all hear now that it was being sung in another language; only none of them knew what language it was. Unaware of Latin words. The voice singing, sound like an elderly male; deep, raspy, it was like he was about to lose his voice at any moment but wanted to sing anyway. The song was slow and drawn out as if he was singing at a funeral. The sound of it gave them all goosebumps, and Torres' butterflies in his stomach grew worse as his nervousness got stronger. He wondered was this just another dream.

Did I fall asleep on the couch? My last dream seemed so vivid and real, what makes this moment any different? This must be another dream. He puts his arms behind his back and begins to pitch himself. Thinking he's dreaming. He didn't want Sarah nor Amy to see what he was doing just in case it was real, but when he broke the skin and felt the pain and blood confirm it for him that he was wide awake. He shook his head in disappointment and tunes back into what was happening. They all stood around the door of the master bedroom and listened to the words of the song. Trying to figure out what language it's from. The song went,

"Occuli mei degluttiat vos vivus, nolo ut occidere vos, suus' easy para vos ut morietur, Ego cupiditatem paulo delectationis et furantur gaudium ille est apud vestra vita, vos autem numquam videre vestra uxorem rursus, ut para dic vale."

Of course, none of them spoke Latin and had no understanding of what was being said,

"That does not sound like Spanish," Amy whispered.

In his mind, Torres agreed with Amy that it wasn't Spanish, but he wasn't going to give Sarah the satisfaction of admitting he was wrong. The singing stops. They stood there and looked at each other for a moment. They were all uneasy, with Amy and Sarah visibly showing their uneasiness, but Torres did his best to hide his. They could feel something was wrong. Sarah leaned on the master bedroom's door and listened. Trying to see if she could hear a commercial playing or even static from the alleged radio.

"This is stupid." Torres scoffed then went for the door.

He grabbed the knob and burst in. Christina sat on the side of the bed, bent over to her knees with her hands covering her face. They all entered the room and surrounded her. Torres's heart dropped to his stomach, he still had a bit of doubt, and they were just overreacting, but seeing was believing. What made it even worse was when he looked at their bedroom chest where the radio is and saw the radio's cord dangling from it, it wasn't even plugged in. The only bright side was at least now he wasn't experiencing the weird behavior alone. He has witnesses.

"Christina, are you ok?" He asked.

Christina mumbles.

"Huh? I can't hear you."

He squats down in front of her and turns his head closer to her trying to make out her mumbles. Suddenly the bedroom door they left open; slams shut. Amy and Sarah both let out a scream, and Torres bolts up to his feet. Christina lets out an agonizing moan as she slowly sits up straight. She holds her head up with her eyes closed and keeps her hands in her lap.

"Christina?" Sarah called.

"Christina, honey, are you alright?" Amy asked.

The sound of Amy's voice causes Christina's eyes to open, exposing those horrible glowing blood-red eyes. They all gasped and backed away at the same time as if it was a reflex.

"Amy…Amy, I told you, I'll see you again."

Christina spoke. Only it wasn't her voice. Amy's heart sank, and a tear fell from her left eye.

"Jared?" Amy utters.

Jared was Amy's ex-husband, the abusive relationship she was in years ago. He was convicted for first-degree domestic violence after brutally beating her with a baseball bat. Claiming that's how he "punishes her." Jared was sentenced to six years but committed suicide after being in prison for six months. Torres and Sarah's eyes widen in shock, unable to believe what they were hearing and seeing. Christina continues in Jared's voice.

"You fat whore!" She yelled.

"No, no, it's impossible! You're dead! You're dead!" Amy shouted hysterically.

Tears were now streaming down her face, Christina stares at Amy with pure hatred in those glowing red eyes. Amy turns away, unable to handle the hateful glare. Christina chuckles as she starts to rock back and forth. She starts to sing again, in Jared's voice, but this time in English,

"My eyes could swallow you alive, No I won't kill you, it's too

easy for you to die, I rather have some fun and steal the joy that's in your life, you'll never see your wife again, so prepare to say good-bye."

Amy backs into a corner and sobs uncontrollably. Before Torres and Sarah could give a reaction, Torres and Christina's king-sized bed violently shakes, causing everything in the room to vibrate. The dresser mirror rattles then shatter. The things on top of dresser fall, glass bottles of cologne and perfume slams to the floor breaking on impact. Christina gets her voice back and starts to laugh hysterically. Suddenly, both Sarah and Torres's noses start to pour blood.

"We got to get out of here!" Sarah yelled.

"NO, CHRISTINA!" Torres cries.

Christina lets out a screech.

Sarah gets the bedroom door open.

"Come on. We got to go!" She urged.

Sarah helped Amy to her feet and pushes her out the door, then turns back to grab Torres, who is now in tears. It broke his heart to see the love of his life has completely lost it. Sarah manages to drag him out into the hallway and closes the bedroom door behind. She darts to the linen closet and grabs two towels to clean up the blood that was all over them.

"Let's go!" Sarah demanded.

"No, no, we got to help her." Torres moan.

He was overwhelmed with different feelings. He could barely breathe through all the blood, and his heart ached with so much emotional pain.

"Listen to me we can't help her, we got to call my dad," Sarah said. "We'll be back, I promise."

She assured. They all left out of the house. Sarah took everyone in her car because Amy was too distraught to drive.

Chapter Twenty-Three

"So how old are you?"

Paul cheerfully asked the young boy next in line.

"I'm nine years old."

The boy answers, staring up at Paul with those bright brown eyes. The church is having its annual "back to school" drive. All summer long people donate money and school supplies for the kids whose parents have trouble buying them. Pastor Henry gets a copy of the list of school supplies commonly needed from all the local schools and takes the donated money to purchase the items on the list that they haven't yet received. Every year the giving increases, making this year the most the church has ever raised so far. Pastor Henry, with the help of his family and other church members along with Paul, were able to get not only the needed supplies but school backpacks to carry them in. The event was held in the church's back yard. They sectioned off different tables for the preschool, elementary, junior high, and high school. Paul was helping in the elementary section.

"What grade are you entering." Paul continues.

"Fourth grade." The boy whispered.

The young boy seemed shy. Paul figured he got his timid personality from his mother, who stood quietly beside him. Paul didn't want to pressure the boy into small talk, so he only had one more question for him.

"Which one would you like?"

He asked, referring to the school backpacks. Each book bag was filled with the needed supplies for that school. The preschool and elementary kid's school backpacks came in a variety of colors, decorated with famous cartoon characters or comic book superheroes. The junior high and high schoolers had a variety of solid colors. The young boy didn't say his answer out loud but pointed to the one he wanted.

"Ah Batman, great choice," Paul said as he handed it to him.

"Matthew, what do you say?"

His mother asked. It was the first time she spoke since Paul greeted her.

"Thank you," Matthew responded.

"You're welcome. Y'all enjoy the rest of your day."

Paul waved them goodbye, and the mother politely acknowledged, but Matthew immediately opens his new backpack and glances at the supplies inside. He was urged by his mom to wait until they got into the car before he went through it, so he wouldn't accidentally drop anything. Pastor Henry was coming out of the church as Matthew, and his mother was about to go in. It was easier to go through the church to get to their car that was parked in front, then maneuvering through the crowd of people and tables to go around the church. Pastor Henry watched the new fourth grader toss the school backpack over his shoulders, smiling and showing off his new bag as if he had just won a prize, seeing his joy gave Pastor Henry joy as well. He continued to watch as the young boy skipped happily ahead of his mother until they both disappeared out the front church doors. ***It's amazing how good it feels to give***. Pastor Henry thought as he realizes for the first time in a while, he's happy. He allows a smile to form on his face and continues outside.

"There you are," Elisabeth said.

Pastor Henry was pleasantly surprised when he walked out the door and was met face to face with his wife. Elisabeth or Lizzy is what he calls her, a nickname he gave her years ago. Friends and family refer to her as "Beth," but Pastor Henry wanted to be different. She was on her way to go into the church to look for him. "

Hiya Lizzy, you looking for me?" He asked.

"Yes, I misplaced my phone. I was about to call Sarah and see what was taking her so long and realized I didn't have it on me. Could you please go check in your office and see if I left it there?"

Pastor Henry didn't want to go. He wanted to be outside helping, not looking for a phone his wife constantly loses.

"If it's in my office, why don't you just go and get it; you have a key." He suggested.

"No dear, I have to get back to my table, besides, you can go in and out faster than I can."

She would go there, he thought. Elisabeth has bad knees and may need surgery for them. They make it difficult to walk or stand for long periods, which is why she is the only one with a stool at her table.

"Ok, honey, go have a seat, and I'll bring it to you."

She smiles then slowly makes her way back to her table. Pastor Henry turns around and heads back inside. The back door of the church is on the far-left side of the altar. He looks down at his watch, and it was fifteen minutes till noon. He to wondered what was taking Sarah so long to arrive. The charitable event started at eleven, but everyone who volunteered arrived thirty minutes earlier, except for Pastor Henry and Elisabeth, who came in at ten. They all had already pre-packed the backpacks and set up the tables the day before, and Sarah was there then. Yet, today over an hour has passed, and she was a no show. ***That's not like her. If she were going to be late, she would have called***. That's when Pastor Henry felt his pockets and realized he too didn't have his phone on him either. So, he doesn't know whether she called or not. Pastor Henry started to pick up the pace. Now he was feeling anxious about neither him nor his wife having their phones on them. Pastor Henry feared something could have happened to Sarah, and she could be calling and letting them know. As he walks through the church, all that could be heard was his heavy breathing as he tried to power walk, but the sound of sniffling and whimpering began to drown him out. Pastor Henry immediately stops walking and looks for the source of the sound, fearing that it was a small child crying. He stood in the middle of the aisle, between the sets of pews on both sides of him. As he pans the room, he finally sees on the very last pew, on his right side, a figure that looked like a woman, sitting there crying.

"Hello, are you alright?!" He calls out.

All he could see was her wild black hair and brown skin tone. She had her head down, so he wasn't able to see her face. She just rocked her body back and forth like she was distraught. As he got closer, he could finally see that she was an Afro American woman.

"Ma'am, are you okay?" Pastor Henry called out again.

Utterly ignoring him, she rocks faster and starts to wail loudly. Her wails gave him goosebumps, but he continues closer to her.

"Hey, ma'am, please calm down, the children might hear you."

He reached the last pew and started to shuffle down the narrow aisle to get over to her when suddenly he feels a hand grasp his shoulder. He quickly turns around, surprised by the touch. It was one of the volunteers. He exhales a sigh of relief, but then looks at her with confusion when he sees the noticeably concerned look on her face.

"Pastor, are you okay?"

She asked in a delicate voice. She was a young college student entering her sophomore year.

"Yes, I'm fine."

Pastor Henry answered, still wondering why she was both looking and talking to him as if something was wrong.

"I just…I heard you shouting. Are you sure you're okay?"

She gently placed her hand on his arm. He, in return, put his hand on top of hers.

"I'm fine, sweetheart, you scared me as all. I was trying to find out what was wrong with this young lady."

The college student looked pass Pastor Henry then around.

"What lady?" She asked.

Pastor Henry inadvertently snatches from her as he quickly turns around. There was no one there.

"She must have left; didn't you hear her crying?"

The college student grabs Pastor Henry's arms with both hands and gently turns him towards her.

"Pastor, I came in shortly after you did, to get more backpacks, and all I saw was you shouting in this direction. I called out to you, but you didn't hear me. So that's when I ran up to you."

"Don't fool around, that's not funny!"

Pastor Henry was angry that she could think that he was making the whole thing up, but when they both saw how serious the other was being, the college student's expression went from concerned to confused, and Pastor Henry's went from bewildered to worried.

"I'm sorry, it must have been a child crying outside, and I mistook the sound to be in here." Pastor Henry changed his tone. "I thought I saw someone, but old age seems to have gotten to me, and my eyesight ain't what it used to be."

He said jokingly, in a weak attempt to lighten the situation. What he really wanted was to walk away from this very awkward moment he was having with the volunteer. He was not only afraid but embarrassed as well. The college student immediately didn't believe his excuse; she had entered the church not but a minute after Pastor Henry began rushing over and shouting at the empty pew, and she never saw nor heard anyone else in there, but them. Even though she wasn't buying his explanation, she could feel the uneasiness coming from him and knew it would be best just to dismiss everything. Of all the time the student has known him, she nor anyone she knows has ever seen him behave like this. So, she decided to accept the idea that Pastor Henry was just having a bad day.

"Could you let Elisabeth know I'll bring her phone out to her shortly?"

"Okay."

She nodded. She went and gathered as many backpacks she could carry, then headed outside. Pastor Henry took one last look around the church, unable to shake the feeling of what he saw, then continued to his office. He felt so uncomfortable and frequently looked over his shoulder. ***Feels like someone is watching me.***

"Is she still here?" He asks himself.

He stood in front of his office door, reaching into his pocket to retrieve his keys. Pastor Henry unlocks the door and takes one last look over his shoulder before he goes inside. Seeing and hearing nothing more, he quickly closes the door behind him. As he walks further in, he sees his and his wife's phone on top of the desk. Grabbing both phones. He pressed the power button on the side of his wife's phone to turn the screen light on, displaying the lock screen, then doing the same to his, turns on the screen light, and sure enough, they both had missed calls from Sarah. He knew he should go and bring Elisabeth her phone since she is waiting for it, but Pastor Henry couldn't shake the urgency he has to know what was keeping Sarah. Pastor Henry puts Elisabeth's phone in his pocket and heads out of his office. He locks his office's door, then pauses, he taps Sarah's missed call and immediately, the phone starts dialing Sarah. As the phone rings, Pastor Henry continues to head back outside. As he gets to the end of the corridor, he glances over at the pew where he last saw the woman sitting, and still, it was empty. Now convinced that maybe his eyes were playing tricks on him and the sound he heard earlier, came from outside. Although highly unlikely because he knows he saw her, there was no doubt in his mind, where did she go? Since that was a question he couldn't answer, Pastor Henry felt it was best to forget the whole thing. He listens as Sarah's voicemail prompt began to play and hangs up. As he searched his phone to try again. He reaches the back door of the church, but before he could leave out the door, he suddenly hears the same sobbing. Without thinking, Pastor Henry turns around, and power walks back to the pew as if he was waiting to hear her again. He was going to prove the sobbing lady exists, not only to himself but to the college student, who didn't believe him. He makes it to the pew, but again no one was there. He put his phone in his pocket, freeing his hands. He dug a finger in each ear to clean them out. He listens. The sobbing continues, but the woman was nowhere in sight. Without freaking out, he calmly walks around the church, trying to find her. He tried to decipher whether the sound was coming from the outside or inside the church. Thinking it had to be from outside since it seems he was the only one inside, but he couldn't ignore how loud and clear her sobbing was, it was like she is standing right beside him. A couple of minutes passed as he walked around the church. Looking under and behind the pews, trying to see if she was hiding from him. When he glanced up at the large curtain covering the baptism pool. The sobbing stopped. It was as if as soon as he noticed the curtain, he found her hiding place, and she was trying to keep quiet, to keep him from finding her. Pastor Henry walks up the pulpit towards the large curtain covering the baptism pool to look behind it. Before he could get to it, he hears a loud thump in the hallway behind him. He quickly turns around and heads in the direction of the thud. Chasing every sound, he hears, trying to find the woman. Obsessed with confronting her because he wanted to assure himself that she's real. Pastor Henry fears if he can't find her, it could mean he's losing his mind. He cautiously makes his way down the hallway, listening closely. He tipped toed like a hunter stalking its prey. There were only four doors in the hallway. The men's and women's bathroom, the utility closet or also known as the "broom closet," and Pastor Henry's office, there was nowhere to hide. He knew no one was in his office because he just left there and locked the door behind him. So that leaves the bathrooms and utility closet to be her potential hiding place. He then realizes if she is hiding in the women's bathroom, he couldn't go in to see, not with today being a busy day, and someone could walk in on him being in there. Trying to explain that he was in the women's bathroom looking for a woman would not end well at all. ***Where else could she be? I can't go in there, I know***

it. He decided to end the game of cat and mouse and accept his loss. He chalked it up to someone playing a very insensitive prank and figured he had already wasted enough time. There was so much to do on this busy day, not to mention he still hasn't learned why Sarah hasn't shown up yet. He again heads his way back to join the charity event. The sudden rattling of the doorknob to the utility closet startles him as he walked past it. ***She's in there.*** He thought as he reaches for the doorknob but stops at the sound of low growls. Pastor Henry jumped, startled by the sudden loud pounding on the door. Like whatever or whoever is in there was trying to break out. The growls got louder; the pounding continued. The doorknob jerked so violently he thought it would soon break. Pastor Henry backs away from the door, dumbfounded. He couldn't believe what he was witnessing. ***Who is this?*** He wondered. He went from a little fearful to terrified. Abruptly everything stopped as quickly as it started, and all was quiet. It seems whatever is in the closet has given up on its escape.

With every ounce of courage, he had left, he reaches for the doorknob. He took in a deep breath, then snatched the door open. Nothing…There was no one or anything in there.

"THAT'S IMPOSSIBLE?!" He yelled, stunned, and slamming the door shut.

Sarah bursts in with her arm around Amy and Torres walks in slowly behind them.

"AH!" Pastor Henry hollered, startled again.

He leaned his body against the utility closet's door. Pastor Henry's fear was making him nauseous, and that last scare almost made him faint. Sarah gently sat Amy down to the first pew they came to.

"Dad, something terrible is wro…Are you alright?" Sarah saw how upset her father was and rushed over to help him stand. "What happened?" She questioned.

"I…I don't know." He stuttered. Pastor Henry couldn't stop trembling.

"Dad, I need to tell you and mom something very important,"

Sarah said as she helped Pastor Henry to his office, and Torres followed. They left Amy inside the church, to let her grieve; Sarah felt she could use some time alone. After Sarah got Pastor Henry seated at his desk, she rushed out the door to get her mother. When they all were together in the office, Sarah began,

"Mom, Dad…do y'all remember my college roommate, Christina?" Both Pastor Henry and Elisabeth searched their thoughts for a second, then vaguely remembered Christina. They have only met her a few times during Sarah's college years then once more at Sarah's wedding.

"Yes, why?" Elisabeth replied.

"Well, she's married to this man, Torres Sosa."

"Yeah, I've met him before, Josh brought him by." Pastor Henry began trying to regain his composure.

"Dad, I think she's possessed. I know she is." Sarah blurted out.

"Possessed?" Pastor Henry and Elisabeth responded at the same time.

"Yes, I don't know the whole story, but I just left their home, and Christina was doing things that can't be explained. I mean, the voice that talked to us wasn't hers, and Amy, the lady that came in with us, she's also Christina's boss. Confirmed that Christina was acting strangely yesterday, and Torres confessed he noticed it too. That's why you left the house last night, isn't it?" Sarah turned to Torres, awaiting a response.

"Yes, she…um, she," Torres was choking back tears. He's heartbroken over his wife's condition.

"Oh dear, Sarah, don't bother him right now, give him a minute." Elisabeth scolded.

"Mom, I'm not trying to be mean, and Torres, I'm sorry. We must do something. We should go get her and bring her here."

"We can't bring her here with all these children here," Elisabeth said. She turns to Pastor Henry,

"Honey, I think you should go to their home and pray for her."

The thought of that made Pastor Henry sick to his stomach. He was already afraid and didn't think he could do it, but all eyes were on him at that moment before he could say anything Sarah's phone rings.

"It's Josh...Hello, babe, listen something has happened, and I will explain everything to you in person, but meet us at Torres's house in twenty minutes, okay. I promise I can better explain everything in person, just meet us there. Bye."

Sarah barely gave Josh time to talk, let alone ask questions, and that was on purpose because she knows Josh would not be quick to go if he knew ahead of time of Christina's possession.

"Dad, Torres, and Josh can hold her down and help you perform an exorcism, that's why I have him meeting us there."

Pastor Henry never answered whether he was going or not, but it looks as if the decision has already been made for him.

"Sarah, you stay here with your mother and help finish the charity." Pastor Henry uttered

"No, Dad, I want to go, she is my friend."

"No, stay here."

"Please, Sarah, the guys can handle this, and we do need your help here. Stay."

Elisabeth chimed in. Sarah reluctantly agreed with her parents but asked to be called if anything went wrong. They all held hands and prayed together before leaving the office. Sarah headed outside to join the charitable event. She substituted for her mother at her table while Elisabeth stayed inside the church with Amy.

"Are you ready, son?" Pastor Henry asked Torres.

Torres nodded his head, "yes." Pastor Henry asked a question he couldn't answer. He didn't want to go but felt he had to. So, they headed out the door to Pastor Henry's pickup truck.

After saying goodbye to the last student in his line, Paul decides to take a short break while he had the chance. Beside the church's back door, were seven large coolers lined up against the church wall—each one filled with ice and bottles of water. Paul reached inside one and grabbed a bottle then headed inside. Although it was a nice cloudy day, it was still humid out, and the humidity had Paul hot and sweaty. He figured he should go to the bathroom, wet some paper towels, and use them to wipe the sweat off his face and neck. As he walked down the aisle, he couldn't help but notice sitting on the last pew on his left side was Elisabeth with her arms around a woman who is very upset. Elisabeth rocks and shushes trying to comfort her.

"Beth, is everything alright?" Paul asks, but before she could answer. The woman she is comforting interrupts.

"No, everything is not alright! Everything is terrible! JUST TERRIBLE!" She yelled.

"I'm sorry, is there anything I could do to help?" Paul kneels next to them.

"Paul, this is Amy, and she just had a traumatic experience but, John is taking care of it," said Elisabeth.

"Are you sure?" Paul asked.

"Yes, Paul, I'm sure, but it's nice of you to be concerned." Elisabeth smiles.

"Okay, if there is anything I can do to help, please let me know."

"Thank you." Elisabeth responds and continues to try to calm down Amy.

Paul stands to his feet and continues to the men's room. When he reached the hallway and out of sight from Elisabeth and Amy, he paused for a moment. Paul couldn't get over how upset Amy was. He was worried, but even more curious to know what the "traumatic experience" was she witnessed. Paul listened as Elisabeth tried desperately to console Amy. He began to feel guilty for eavesdropping and continued, but before he could walk through the bathroom door, Elisabeth's voice caught his attention.

"Amy honey, maybe y'all were mistaken. Christina could have a mental illness."

Amy pulled away from Elisabeth. She looked her straight in the eyes and stared at her with a shocked expression.

"Mental illness? Amy began. Are you serious? Christina spoke to me in my DEAD. HUSBAND'S. VOICE!" She shouted.

"Amy, please, there are kids nearby, and you don't want them to hear you!" Elisabeth hushed.

"Well, stop talking to me like I'm crazy! That's not a mental illness. Christina's possessed!"

Paul gasped. Those words "Christina's possessed" hit him like a bolt of lightning. Casting out a devil is what he is called to do, his dream, his epiphany all led to that moment. Paul knew immediately he had to know who Christina is and where she was. He jogged back over to Amy and Elisabeth.

"Beth, please, you have to tell me about Christina."

Chapter Twenty-Four

As Pastor Henry and Torres were approaching the Sosa's residence, they saw Josh's black pickup truck parked in Torres' driveway, so Pastor Henry pulls in behind him. Seeing them arrive, Josh hops out his vehicle and walks over to the driver's side before Pastor Henry could turn off his truck. ***Torres has been acting strange lately; the weird early morning phone call asking for money, he doesn't show up for work this morning, and now Sarah telling me to rush over here without any explanation as to why.*** Josh's mind was overloaded with questions and felt if no one gives him answers soon; his head was going to explode.

"So, anybody going to tell me what's going on?"

Josh asked as soon as Pastor Henry and Torres exited the truck. Torres gave Josh a blank stare, unsure of how to respond. Pastor Henry reached into his back seat to retrieve his bible.

"So, is anybody going to tell me?" He repeated. Torres could see that Josh was growing impatient and finally spoke,

"Something's wrong with Christina."

"Ok, what's wrong?" Josh continued.

Torres froze, the words trapped in his throat. He wished what was happening to Christina, happened to him instead of her. It pained him to see her like this.

"Sarah and Torres both think an evil spirit is plaguing Christina." Pastor Henry answered. He saw how Torres struggled to get his words out and decided to speak up.

"Are you serious?!" Josh exclaimed. That wasn't the answer he expected.

"And you don't think she's possessed?" Torres snaps at Pastor Henry after hearing him say only he and Sarah thinks an evil spirit plagues Christina.

"I think…" Pastor Henry begins, "I think there's a rational explanation for everything."

"So, you think we made all this shit up. You think I would lie about something like that. That's my wife, man, my wife!"

"Hold on, man, just calm down, I don't think he meant anything by it."

Josh puts his arm around Torres's shoulders, trying to calm his friend. Pastor Henry could hear the pain in Torres' voice. He looked at him then turned away, unable to bear the sad expression on his face.

"Come on. You guys, let's just go see what's going on."

Josh said as he walks with Torres up the steps of his porch, and Pastor Henry followed behind. All three stood at the front door, Torres in the middle, Josh on his right, and Pastor Henry on the left. Torres unlocks and opens the door, then pushes it wide open.

"What is that smell, man?" Josh asked.

As soon as they opened the door, they were all hit with a foul scent.

"Smells like sulfur." Pastor Henry answered.

They all stood at the door looking inside and listening. Torres walks inside, follow by Pastor Henry, and Josh enters last closing the door behind him.

The house was silent. No more singing. No sound of movement.

"Christina?" Torres called. No answer.

They searched every room downstairs. Torres also checked the back door making sure it was still locked. Seeing the back door was unbothered, and there was no sign of her downstairs. Pastor Henry suggested for Torres and Josh to go upstairs and bring Christina down into the living room. Pastor Henry went to sit on the sofa as he waited for them to return. Pastor Henry sat there, motionless with the bible on his lap. To say he was anxious being there was an understatement. Pastor Henry felt the same uneasiness he had in church with that crying woman. Who, he was unable to find, and he still has the same feeling of being watched, yet no one was around.

Torres ascended the stairs first, and Josh slowly trailed behind. When they reached the second floor, Torres continues to the master bedroom then paused when he notices Josh wasn't behind him. Josh stood at the top of the stairs, not wanting to go any further.

"Come on, man, I might need your help!" Torres yelled.

"Go ahead; see what she's doing first; she might come downstairs willingly."

Torres shook his head in frustration, but deep down, he could understand Josh's hesitation. Torres just wanted all of this to be over and hoped Pastor Henry could help. He took in a deep breath and opened the door to the master bedroom.

"Christina?"

The room was a mess: the broken perfume and cologne bottles on the floor. The dresser mirror shattered, and the dresser itself flipped upside down. The bedroom's chest was on its side, the mattress was on the floor, and the box spring stood up vertically against the headboard. The white carpet stained with blood from Torres', and Sarah's nosebleed from earlier.

"Christina?"

Torres walked through the mess to check the walk-in closet. Seeing no sign of her, he turns around and notices the scratches on the master bathroom door.

The long claw marks looked as if a wild animal scratched at it, leaving it splintered. He walked over to the bathroom door. He turns his head and rests an ear on it. Listening to see if anyone was in there, but he heard nothing. He swung the door open. Empty. Torres closed the bathroom door and headed out of the master bedroom.

"What happened?" Josh questioned.

"She's not in here."

Torres frantically checked the other rooms upstairs, worried that Christina must have left the house. After searching for Christina in the last bedroom, there was still no sign of her. In a panic, Torres jogs out of the spare room to tell Josh, who was still standing at the top of the stairs, that Christina wasn't here.

"Josh,"

But before Torres could get the words out, he watched as Josh's body lurches back, and he falls backward down the stairs. It looked like someone yanked him down from behind, but there was no one there.

"JOSH!"

Pastor Henry jumps, startled, from the commotion, then runs

out of the living room to see what had happened. Torres runs down the stairs to Josh's aid.

"Josh, Josh, are you alright!" Torres kneels beside his friend.

"What happened? Where's Christina?" Pastor Henry questioned.

"I don't know. Christina's not upstairs." Torres answered.

Josh groans. He landed hard on his back and dislocated his shoulder.

"Ah shit, ugh!" Josh moans.

Torres helps Josh to his feet, then helps pops Josh's shoulder back in place.

"What the fuck just happen!" Josh yelled.

"You tripped down the stairs," said Pastor Henry.

"Pastor, I did not trip; somebody pulled me down."

"Yeah, I saw how he fell, he was just standing there, and then all of a sudden something snatches him down." Torres cosigned. "You going to be okay?"

"I guess, but we got to get the fuck out of here!"

"Josh, you can leave if you want, but I got to find my wife."

"You said she wasn't here, so we have to leave anyway to go and look for her."

Torres ran into the living room, where he left Christina's purse and shoes, the ones Amy brought over, on the coffee table. He looked inside Christina's purse and found her keys. He came back out into the hallway to show Josh and Pastor Henry.

"Look, the front door was locked when we got here, and the back door is still locked as well. Honestly, I don't even think I locked the door behind me when we ran out of here. So, I think…"

"TORRES!"

Josh screamed, interrupting Torres. Torres's eyes widen at the terrified looks on Josh and Pastor Henry's faces. He looked down towards the direction Josh was pointing. To his horror, he was standing in mid-air. Torres didn't even notice that his feet had left the floor. As soon as Torres looks back up at them, his body is suddenly thrown and slams against the wall. Torres was unconscious before he hits the floor. Josh and Pastor Henry took steps towards him but immediately stopped when they heard,

"Tore-ressssss, Tore-ressssss,"

It was Christina, and every time she said Torres' name, she hissed. Christina slowly crept out the kitchen. Both Josh and Pastor Henry backed away. They both looked at each other. They knew they checked everywhere downstairs, and she was nowhere in sight. They didn't hear the back door open or close, and Pastor Henry was sure the only sound he heard while he waited downstairs was the sound of Josh crashing down. Where did she come from? Christina slowly made her way out the kitchen in full sight, walking on her hands and feet like a four-legged animal and leaving speared trails of blood behind. Her fingers on both hands were ripped and bleeding. Pastor Henry leaned forward and squinted his eyes to observe her hands closer. He saw on her left hand, the one more visible from where he stood, that her index, middle, and ring finger were missing its fingernail. Christina's nails were torn completely off. Not able to see her right hand, judging from the amount of blood, he could only assume that it looked identical to the left. Christina crawled over to Torres's unconscious body, where she stops and starts sniffing him like a dog. Pastor Henry and Josh stood shocked and horrified; neither of them has ever witnessed anything like this before.

Paul urged to Beth that he could be of assistance to Pastor Henry, and with hesitation, she finally agreed to allow him to leave his table at the charity event, and she would take his place. Paul got the address to the Sosa's residence from Sarah, typed it in his phone's GPS, and was on his way. The adrenaline pumped through him, but he was not afraid. Paul knew this day was coming but he wasn't expecting it so soon and felt unprepared.

"I don't believe in coincidences. Christina is the one I am called to help."

Paul assures himself. He tried to stay as calm as he could, increasing and decreasing his speed, trying to avoid getting pulled over for speeding. Paul checked the ETA on his GPS and saw he was a mile and a half away.

"I'm almost there."

He became ready for the war ahead of him. Paul starts singing a worship song to the Lord. As he sang, he began to feel his Monte Carlo start to slow to a stop.

"No, Monty, no, not now."

He steered the car off the road onto the grass so that it wouldn't block traffic on the two-lane road. The Monte Carlo turned completely off like all the power in its battery was drained. Paul let out an exaggerated sigh and shook his head. ***Figures Monty would break down when I'm in a hurry.*** The car was off, but he still turned the ignition to the **OFF** position and put it in park. Paul exited the vehicle feeling an urgency in his spirit and knew even if he wanted to wait for a tow truck. He couldn't. There was no time to lose. So, he decided to continue on foot. He checked the GPS to get a grasp of the directions. The two-way road was in a residential area. It was the one road for this neighborhood that the residents used to travel back and forth to the city. Paul stood in the grass in front of his disable Monte Carlo. To the right of him was a wooded area about a mile long. On the other side of the tall trees, weeds, and bushes were more houses. As he studied his phone, he could hear the snapping of twigs and the rustling of bushes coming from the wooded area beside him. Paul wasn't alarmed at all by the sound. It wasn't uncommon for the locals to go through the woods as a shortcut, and there was a convenience store half a mile down the road. He thought it could have been locals passing by or even an animal like a rabbit. Satisfied with his understanding of the direction, Paul turns back to his car to make sure he had locked the doors then continues towards the Sosa's, but as soon as he turned around, he shivered as a cold chill ran through his body. Something he would have immediately ignored if it was cold or even cool outside, but it was nowhere near. It was still as hot and humid as it was when Paul was at church. Suddenly he hears a loud crack, the sound a splinted tree would make right as it was about to fall. This caught his attention to investigate the woods. Standing twenty feet away from him was a large, black, featureless figure. It stood about seven feet tall, it had a wide body, yet no physical looking arms or legs. It was like the silhouette or shadow of André the Giant. Even though it had no eyes, Paul could tell it was staring at him. It is after two o'clock in the afternoon, the bright sun lite up the woods, yet no light illuminated the figure. It was so dark that even the light surrounding it dimmed. Immediately Paul was unnerved by the sight of it. It takes a lot to scare him, but the intense hate that came from it seems to fill the air, and Paul couldn't help but be nervous.

"She's mine," it uttered.

The sound of its distorted roar caused Paul to shiver again. He then realized what it said and understood the situation.

She's mine…Christina. The enemy is trying to intimidate me.

He thought. Paul regained his courage and glared back at the figure.

"The God I serve said, Let not your heart be troubled, neither let it be afraid!" (John 14:27 KJV) He yelled with authority. "I rebuke you in the name of Jesus!"

Suddenly a gust of wind blew through the woods and the light where the figure stood return to normal…it was gone. Paul felt he had wasted enough time; that was a warning he needs to get to the Sosa's as soon as possible. He takes off running and hauls ass down the road.

Josh's breathing grew faster as fear consumed him; all he could do is stare at his longtime friend. Looking back on his friendship with Christina, he never realized he'd known her almost as long as he has known Torres. His mind flashbacks to their high school days, Torres had a huge crush on Christina and used to talk about her all the time. Josh could still see the grin Torres had on his face when Christina agreed to go out with him. He now understands Torres' pain. Josh gets why Torres blew up at Pastor Henry and why Torres is so desperate to help Christina. Josh couldn't imagine what he would do in his position if it had happened to Sarah. Nothing he has ever been through could prepare him for this. Snapping out of his train of thought, Josh looks over at Pastor Henry and finally gains the courage to speak.

"Pastor, I think it's time for some holy water or something."

Pastor Henry looks at Josh to acknowledge him but said nothing; his heart was beating out of his chest. ***I'm not ready for this.*** He was overwhelmed but again felt all eyes were on him. He knew he had to do something. Pastor Henry was trying to relax.

"Christina!" Pastor Henry called.

Christina stops sniffing Torres, whips her head towards the sound of Pastor Henry's voice as if she was startled by it. Pastor Henry paused for a moment and watched her. She turned facing them and stood up straight. Josh directed his attention to Torres's unconscious body, looking directly at Christina was unbearable for him because of her glowing red eyes. However, Pastor Henry couldn't look away. He wanted to be ready. Just in case, she made any false moves. To his surprise, she just stood there looking all around as if she was lost. She then focusses her gaze on Pastor Henry.

"Chri…" Pastor Henry attempted to call her again.

"John?" Christina interrupted.

Christina had given Pastor Henry a false sense of hope. Pastor Henry judged from Christina's demeanor that she was lucid enough to talk to, and thought she was just afraid. He figured a demon wouldn't respond to her name. It would announce its presence and boast the person you see is no longer in control. For a moment, he thought it was her, that everything could be explained away, that they were all just overreacting. Maybe all she needed was some psych help, and the proper medication and her glowing red eyes were just his terrified mind playing tricks on him. Pastor Henry felt foolish for thinking this way, but what's wrong with wishful thinking. Well, all his rational thought came to a halt when Christina spoke. She didn't respond in her voice, but in Pastor Henry's dead father's voice. It was then Pastor Henry realized it wasn't her name it was responding to but the sound of his voice.

"John…son, is that you?" She continued.

Hearing his father's voice immediately broke his heart. It was a reminder of that day. The day he couldn't save his father. The day he lost his faith. Josh has only met Sarah's grandfather briefly a couple of times. Not enough to recognize his voice. However, the fact that Christina was speaking in a man's voice was unnerving.

"John-boy, is that you, son?" She said again, mockingly.

Tears streamed down Pastor Henry's face. The bible he was carrying dropped from his hands, like the weight of it had increased, and he could no longer hold it. Pastor Henry left the bible on the floor, turned his back against the wall, and slid down to the floor, holding himself as he continued to weep like a child needing their blankie. This caused Christina to laugh. Her voice is changing in mid chuckle, from Pastor Henry's father's voice to her own. Josh saw the defeated look on Pastor Henry's face. It was like he would snap at any given minute and have a nervous breakdown. Josh wanted to console him but was too afraid to move. With Pastor Henry at his breaking point, and Torres still unconscious, he knew he was in this alone. His heart pounding was deafening. He needed a way to escape, but Christina was in the way of both exits. To get to the front door, Josh would have to pass her. The back door was through the kitchen at the left of her. Either way, Josh would have to get close to Christina to escape. Going anywhere near her was out of the question.

Josh felt Christina's hateful glare and gave in to her stare, making eye contact with her. Immediately a tear fell from his right eye when he looked into those glowing red eyes. She smirks like she can smell his fear. She crouched back down on her hands and soles of her feet. Suspecting what was next, Josh turns and dashes up the stairs as Christina came charging at him. He darted into the first room he got to on the second floor, which was one of the spare bedrooms, slamming the door shut and locking it. Everything was quiet. Josh rested his body against the door while he tried to catch his breath. Even though his body still ached from his previous fall, the adrenaline that sparked in him to survive numbed the pain. He gathered his thoughts, trying to think of a way to get out of there. A light bulb went off in his mind to call the police and hope that they could help at least restrain Christina. He reached in his pocket for his phone. Thinking calling the police is a great idea only to get punched in the face by fate when he saw his battery was dead.

"You gotta be fucking kidding me!" Josh shouted.

He threw his phone to the floor. Suddenly loud pounding began throughout the house, causing it to shake like an earthquake was hitting it. At least a four on the Richter Scale. Each pound made Josh jump in fear. He was starting to panic and began to get hysterical.

"Oh God, don't let me die like this. I gotta get out of here!" He quivered.

Torres groans, his vision blurry. He manages to sit up and rubs his eyes.

"Oh, fuck!"

He gets his eyes to focus and looks around. He doesn't see any sign of Christina. He sees Pastor Henry sitting on the floor, staring blankly at the wall in front of him, clearly spaced out. Torres staggers to his feet with a massive headache and makes it over to Pastor Henry before falling back onto the floor.

"Hey, Pastor, are you alright?"

Torres asked, shaking Pastor Henry's arm, trying to get him to direct his attention on him and off the wall. Pastor Henry looks at him like Torres just pulled him out of a trance.

"I can't. I can't help you." Pastor Henry said with tears in his eyes.

"What happened, where's Josh? Where's Christina?"

Torres questioned, but Pastor Henry couldn't answer, all he could do was shake his head "no" continuously. Torres wanted to slap Pastor Henry back to his senses but then he hears rapid knocking at his front door. Thinking it was Josh, Torres makes it back to his feet, he stumbles a little from the pain of his head injury but carries on. Torres gets to the front door and opens it to see a man standing there who wasn't Josh.

"Hey…I'm…I'm Paul." Paul was winded, from sprinting that mile. Torres was surprised to see him, but a strange feeling of relief flooded him at the sight of Paul.

"What am I going to do?" Josh whined.

He sat with his back against the door, holding his legs in a fetal position. At his most desperate moment, Josh tried to go out the second floor window, but couldn't get it to open. It was like it was nailed shut. Even when he took a combat boot to it, stomping at it as hard as he could. Every time the window would crack, it would fix itself. He couldn't get it to break completely. It was clear the forces in that house did not want him to leave. Growls began to roar outside the bedroom door. Josh jumps to his feet and backs away from the door. He was breathing like he was having an asthma attack. The growls stopped, and all is quiet again. Josh's heart sank when the feeling he was no longer alone came over him. He turned his head slightly to look behind. Right on the wall, Christina crawled with ease. She was able to crawl across the wall as easily as you walk across the floor. Her face darkened with bruises. She gritted her teeth, snarling at him. As soon as Josh took a step forward to head to the door, she pounces on him. Josh screams and cries for help, but the sound of his cries turn to gasp as Christina began to choke him.

Before Paul could talk to Torres to see what was going on, he was interrupted by Josh's terrifying scream. Without hesitation, Paul took off, running in the direction of the cry, and Torres followed as fast as he could behind him.

"Help! Somebody, PLEASE!"

Josh got out one last call as Christina's grip around his throat got tighter.

In one swift bang, Paul burst through the bedroom door. There he saw Christina on top of Josh choking him.

"NO!" Paul goes and wraps his arms around Christina. "I CAST YOU OUT, IN NAME OF JESUS CHRIST!"

Christina screams, losing her grip on Josh.

Paul continues to pray, "Dear Lord, heal this woman from the damage caused by that foul spirit. I rebuke every devil in this house. I plead the blood of the lamb. Evil spirit, leave this woman, and never come back!" Christina's screams continued. "Lord, I ask you to heal and comfort everyone who has been affected, in Jesus' name, I pray Amen."

Christina seizes violently. She stops and collapses in Paul's arms. The bruises on her face fade until there are completely gone. Torres goes over to them; he touches Christina's face and saw how calm she looked.

"Christina?" He whispered.

She slowly opens her eyes. They were back to normal. No more red discoloration. No more glow. Torres grins from ear to ear. ***It's over.***

"Thank you so much," Torres said to Paul.

"No, no, it wasn't me, thank God," Paul answered.

"Thank you, God! Bless you, Lord Jesus!" Torres cried.

Tears fell from Torres' eyes. It was like a weight has been lifted off his chest. His prayers have been answered, and his heart healed. Torres stares at Christina in awe, and Paul continues to cradle her in his arms.

"Oh, my God!" Josh shouted. Breaking the silence in the room. "I will never miss another church service again!"

Chapter Twenty-Five

Deliverance

-One week Later-

Nanja reaches up to the top of the door frame and feels for Agali's spare key. Finding it, she unlocks the front door of Agali's home and is immediately slapped in the face with the foul smell of decomposing flesh. As Nanja walked further into the house, she saw Madam Jay's lifeless body on the floor. With her hand still grasping her chest, rigor mortis locked her in that position. Nanja took a moment to study the body. There were no visible open wounds or marks on Madam Jay's body. Nanja figured from the position Madam Jay was in, that she must have died from a heart attack. Nanja continues, a trail of dried blood smeared across the floor, lead to the kitchen. As she followed the trail of blood, the smell grew stronger, and the buzzing of flies was apparent. When she reached the kitchen, lying on the floor was Agali. His eyes were gauge and had claw marks around the sockets, one of his legs shaped like an uppercase "L" from the knee down. His arms were out of the shoulder's joint sockets and, his entire torso ripped open, covered with the same claw marks that were around his eye sockets. His intestines were on the floor beside him covered with maggots. Nanja looked amazed at all the gore in front of her. She grins.

"I told you, someone always perishes from that spell." She uttered.

"Hey babe, come here for a sec!" Christina yelled. She's standing in the one spare bedrooms, the one they made into mini storage.

"What's wrong?" Torres asked as he entered the room.

"Babe, remember that brown leather bible my grandmother gave me?"

"Yeah, what about it?"

"Help me go through these boxes and find it."

"Alright, love,"

Torres agreed and started going through the top box of the three stacked boxes in front of him. He stops searching a moment and looks up at Christina, who was waist-deep inside a box.

"Christina, how are you feeling?" He asked.

"I'm feeling a lot better." She responded, still searching for her bible.

"You would tell me if anything is wrong, right?"

Christina stops her search and stands up straight. She locks eyes with him,

"Torres, after what we been through, I promise to share everything with you."

Torres walks over to her and gives Christina a warm embrace. He grabs her face with the intent to kiss her when a flash of lights catches his attention. They're standing in front of the window. The half-closed curtain allowed the flashing lights of the police cars to enter the room. Torres steps away from Christina to peer out the window for a closer look, and she too stands beside him and looks out.

"Whoa, isn't that the depressed-looking lady from the night we went to Agali's house for dinner?"

Torres asked, referring to Nanja, who was standing on what used to be Agali's front doorsteps, talking to the police.

"Yeah, that's his sister," Christina remembered.

"Yo, check out the back of that guy's jacket, it says, "Coroner." That means there's a dead body. Agali must be dead!" Torres exclaimed then looks at Christina.

She returns his gaze and asks… "I wonder what happened?"

Made in the USA
Monee, IL
10 August 2021

75413304R00132